Cat & Cat

PAPERCUT**Z**

MORE GREAT GRAPHIC NOVEL SERIES AVAILABLE FROM

PAPERCUTZ™

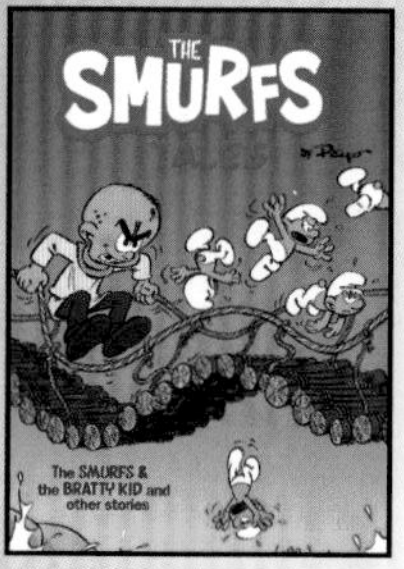
THE SMURFS TALES
The SMURFS & the BRATTY KID and other stories
PAPERCUTZ
THE SMURFS TALES

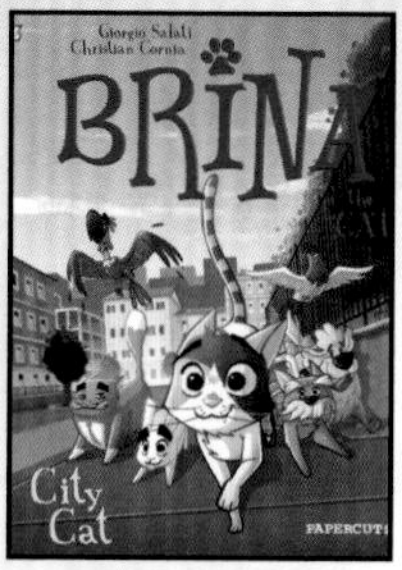
Giorgio Salati
Christian Cornia
BRINA
City Cat
PAPERCUTZ
BRINA THE CAT

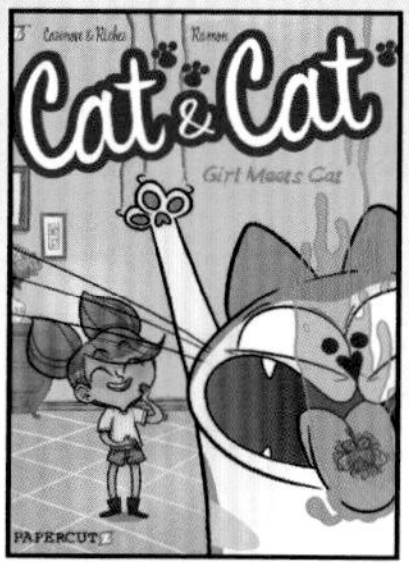
Cazenove & Richez
Ramon
Cat & Cat
Girl Meets Cat
PAPERCUTZ
CAT & CAT

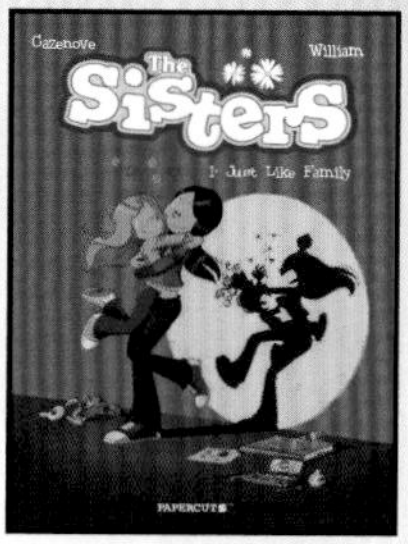
Cazenove
William
The Sisters
1. Just Like Family
PAPERCUTZ
THE SISTERS

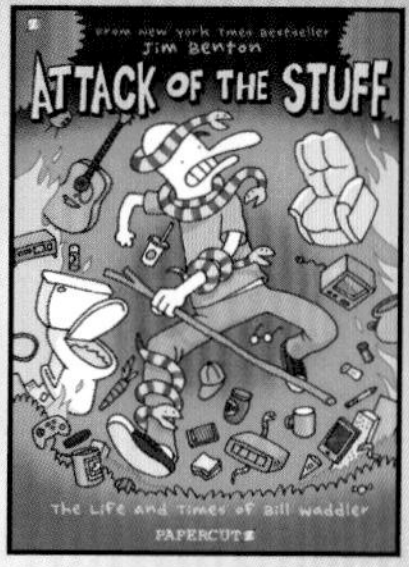
from new york times bestseller
Jim Benton
ATTACK OF THE STUFF
The Life and Times of Bill Waddler
PAPERCUTZ
ATTACK OF THE STUFF

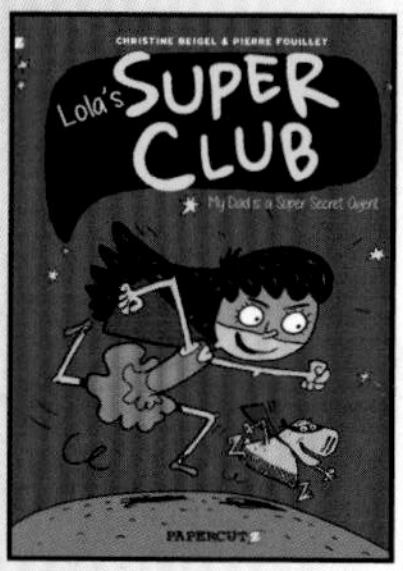
CHRISTINE BEIGEL & PIERRE FOUILLET
Lola's SUPER CLUB
My Dad is a Super Secret Agent
PAPERCUTZ
LOLA'S SUPER CLUB

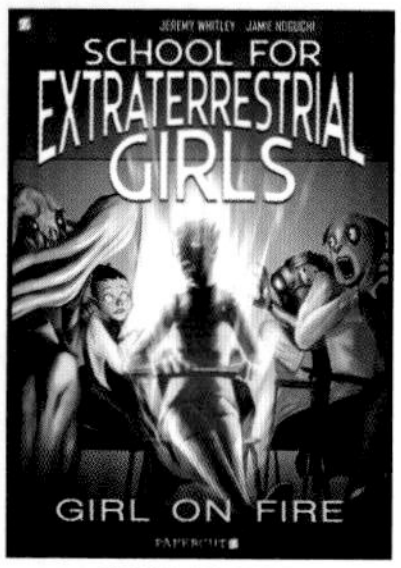
JEREMY WHITLEY · JAMIE NOGUCHI
SCHOOL FOR EXTRATERRESTRIAL GIRLS
GIRL ON FIRE
PAPERCUTZ
SCHOOL FOR EXTRATERRESTRIAL GIRLS

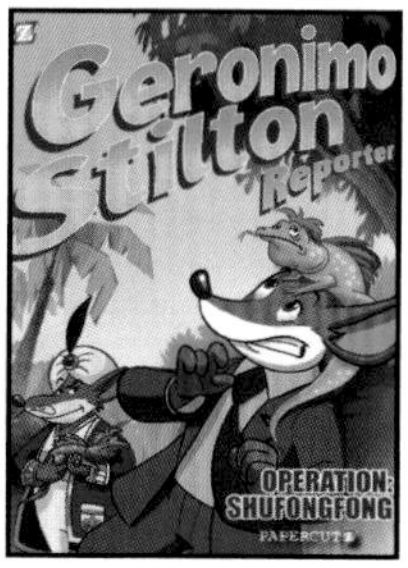
Geronimo Stilton
Reporter
OPERATION: SHUFONGFONG
PAPERCUTZ
GERONIMO STILTON REPORTER

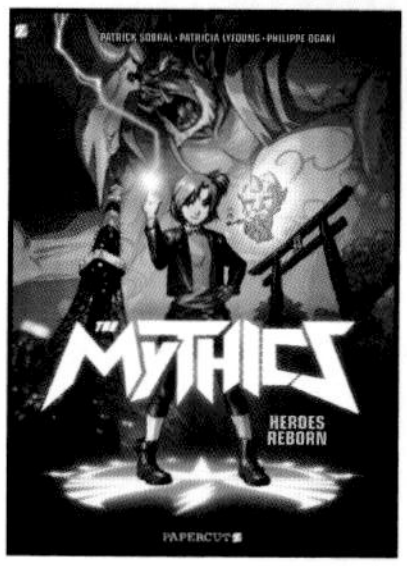
THE MYTHICS
HEROES REBORN
PAPERCUTZ
THE MYTHICS

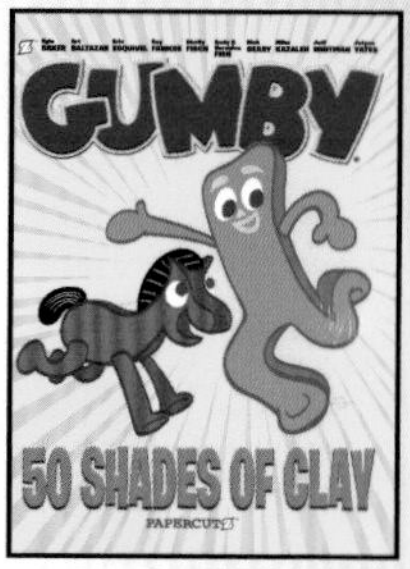
GUMBY
50 SHADES OF CLAY
PAPERCUTZ
GUMBY

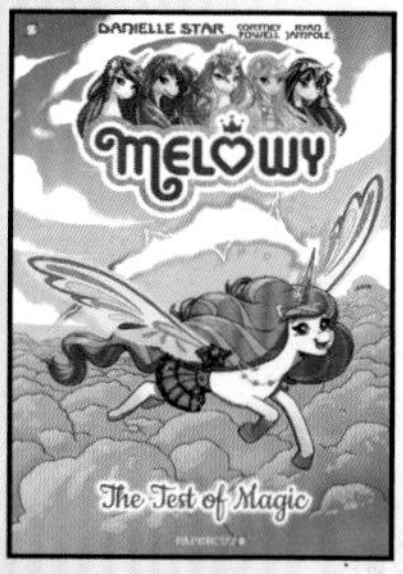
DANIELLE STAR
MELOWY
The Test of Magic
PAPERCUTZ
MELOWY

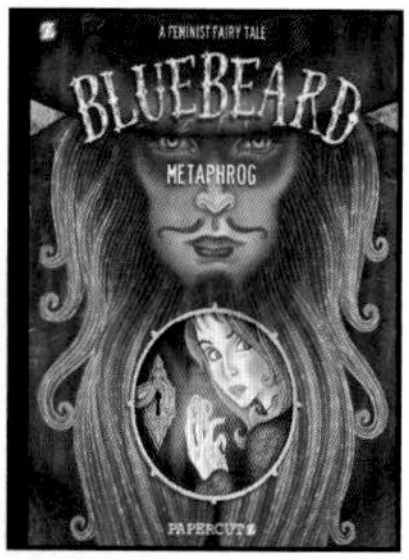
A FEMINIST FAIRY TALE
BLUEBEARD
METAPHROG
PAPERCUTZ
BLUEBEARD

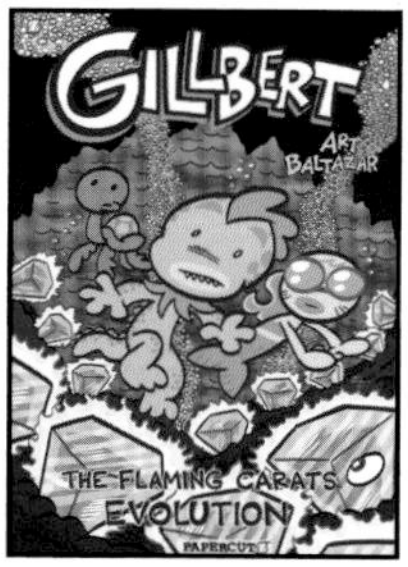
GILLBERT
ART BALTAZAR
THE FLAMING CARATS EVOLUTION
PAPERCUTZ
GILLBERT

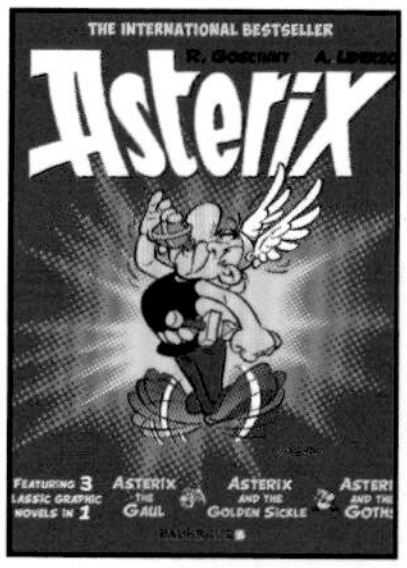
THE INTERNATIONAL BESTSELLER
Asterix
ASTERIX THE GAUL
ASTERIX AND THE GOLDEN SICKLE
ASTERIX

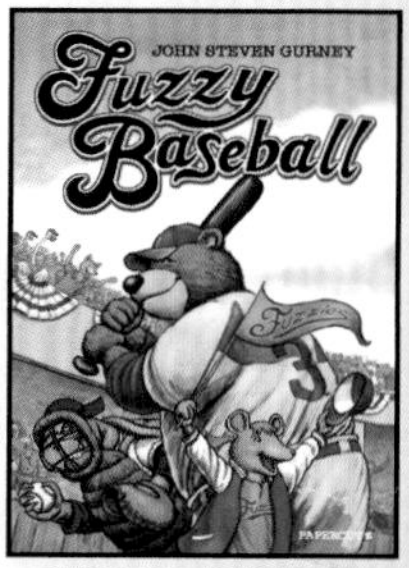
JOHN STEVEN GURNEY
Fuzzy Baseball
PAPERCUTZ
FUZZY BASEBALL

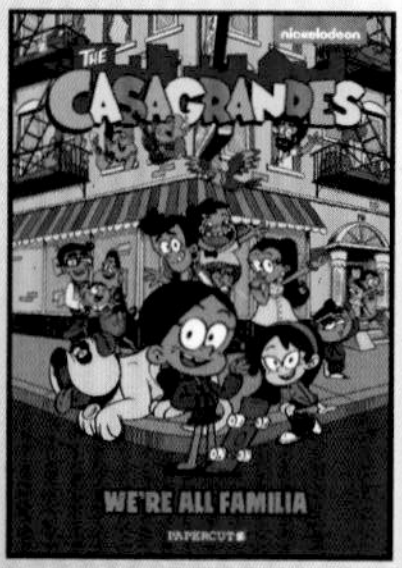
nickelodeon
THE CASAGRANDES
WE'RE ALL FAMILIA
PAPERCUTZ
THE CASAGRANDES

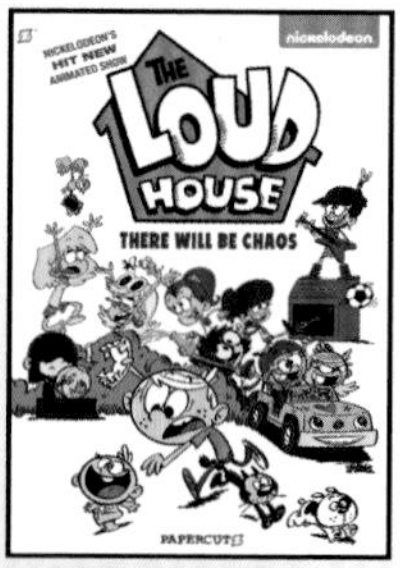
nickelodeon
THE LOUD HOUSE
THERE WILL BE CHAOS
PAPERCUTZ
THE LOUD HOUSE

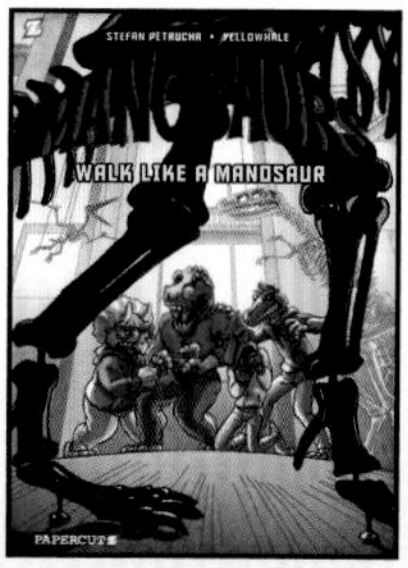
MANOSAURS
WALK LIKE A MANOSAUR
PAPERCUTZ
MANOSAURS

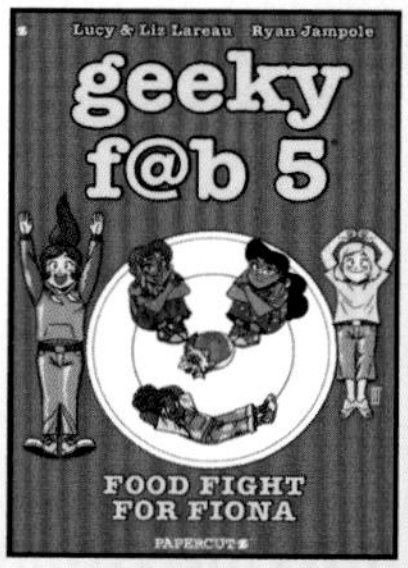
Lucy & Liz Lareau
Ryan Jampole
geeky f@b 5
FOOD FIGHT FOR FIONA
PAPERCUTZ
GEEKY F@B 5

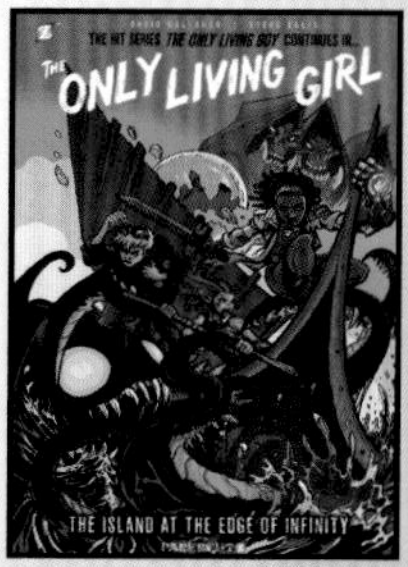
THE ONLY LIVING GIRL
THE ISLAND AT THE EDGE OF INFINITY
THE ONLY LIVING GIRL

papercutz.com

Also available where ebooks are sold.

Cat & Cat

4. SCAREDY CAT

  CHRISTOPHE CAZENOVE
HERVÉ RICHEZ
SCRIPT

YRGANE RAMON
ART

 YRGANE RAMON
JOÃO MOURA
COLOR

 **PAPERCUTZ**
New York

To my parents,

To Shadow, Tsatsiki, Lotus, and Pixel.
To the late Toudougras AKA Zigouingouin.
To La grisette, Jeannot, Villard & Minette.
To friends, readers, and all the cats who bring this series to life.
To Pierre.
Thanks.

Bye Bye Toudougras
2003 to 2017

– Thanks to Pierre Leloup for the preparation for colorization of the first half of this book.
A huge thanks to João Moura for the coloring of the characters in the second half of this volume.

www.joaomouraart.com

– Yrgane

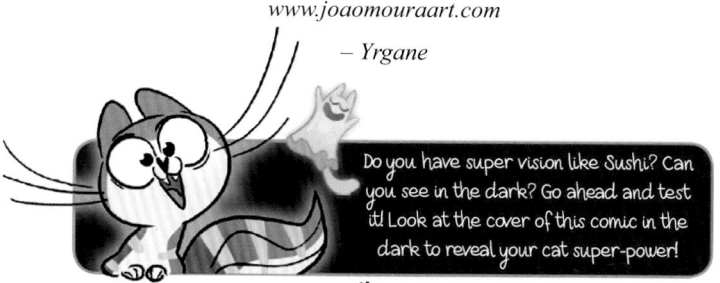

Do you have super vision like Sushi? Can you see in the dark? Go ahead and test it! Look at the cover of this comic in the dark to reveal your cat super-power!

Cat & Cat

#4 "Scaredy Cat"
Christophe Cazenove &
Hervé Richez — Writers
Yrgane Ramon — Artist, Colorist
João Moura — Colorist
Joe Johnson — Translator
Wilson Ramos Jr. — Letterer

Special thanks to Catherine Loiselet

Production — Mark McNabb
Managing Editor — Jeff Whitman
Jim Salicrup
Editor-in-Chief

Papercutz books may be purchased for business or promotional use. For information on bulk purchases please contact Macmillan Corporate and Premium Sales Department at
(800) 221-7945 x5442.

Hardcover ISBN: 978-1-5458-0700-2
Paperback ISBN: 978-1-5458-0701-9

Printed in Turkey
Elma Basım
July 2021

Distributed by Macmillan
First Papercutz Printing

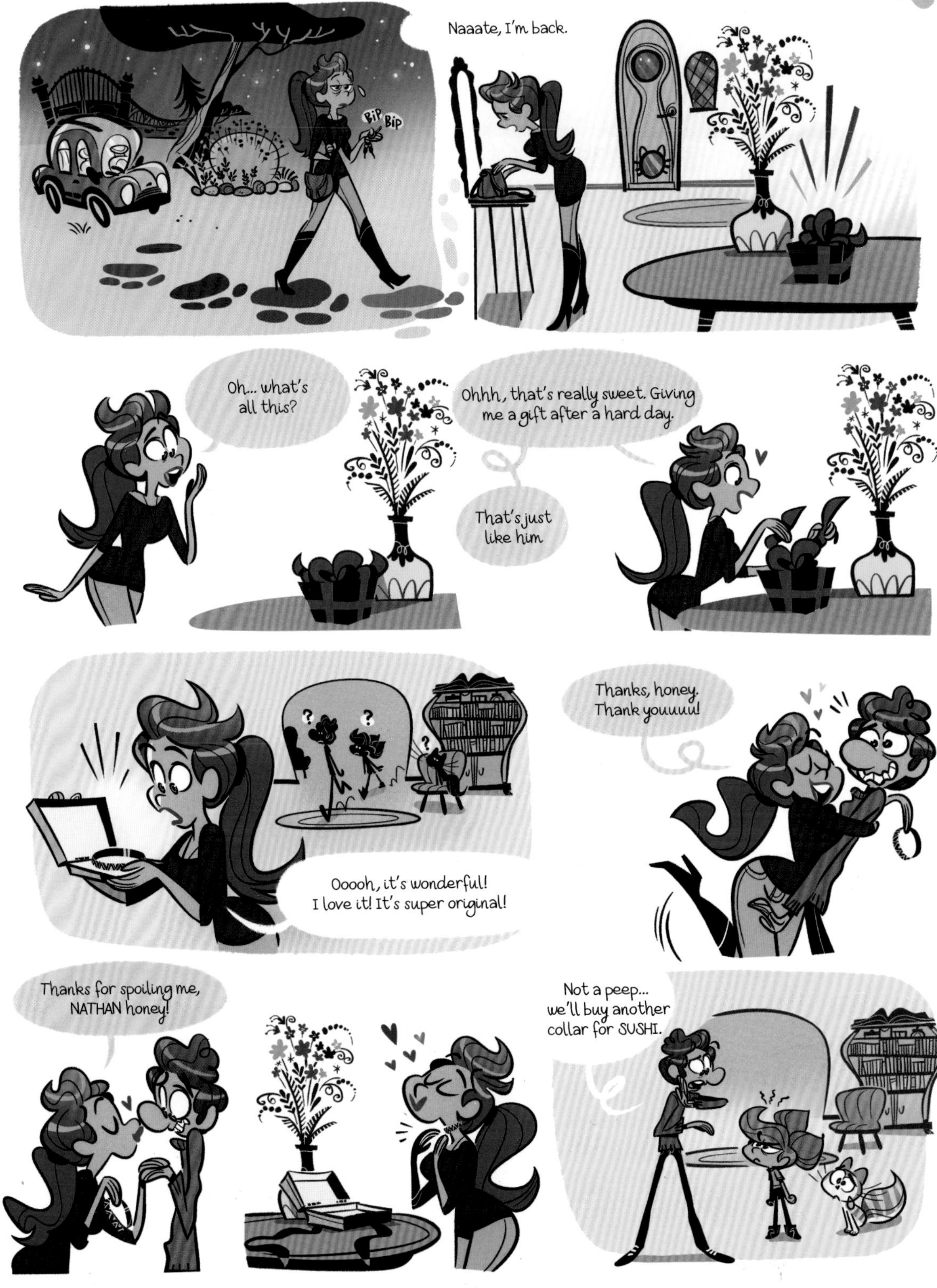
BIP BIP
Naaate, I'm back.
Oh... what's all this?
Ohhh, that's really sweet. Giving me a gift after a hard day.
That's just like him
Ooooh, it's wonderful! I love it! It's super original!
Thanks, honey. Thank youuuu!
Thanks for spoiling me, NATHAN honey!
Not a peep... we'll buy another collar for SUSHI.

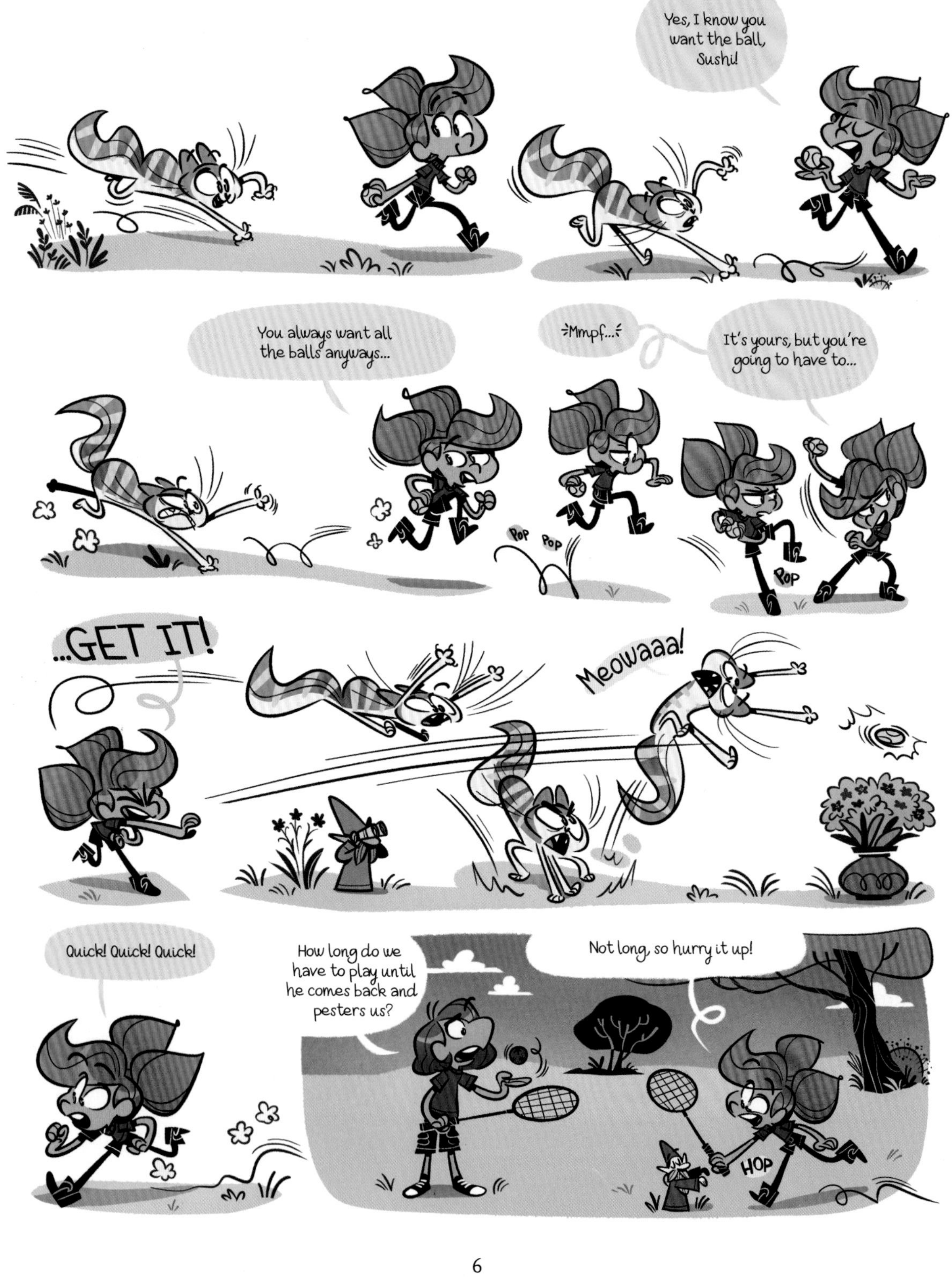
Yes, I know you want the ball, Sushi!
You always want all the balls anyways...
Mmpf...
It's yours, but you're going to have to...
POP
POP
POP
...GET IT!
Meowaaa!
Quick! Quick! Quick!
How long do we have to play until he comes back and pesters us?
Not long, so hurry it up!
HOP

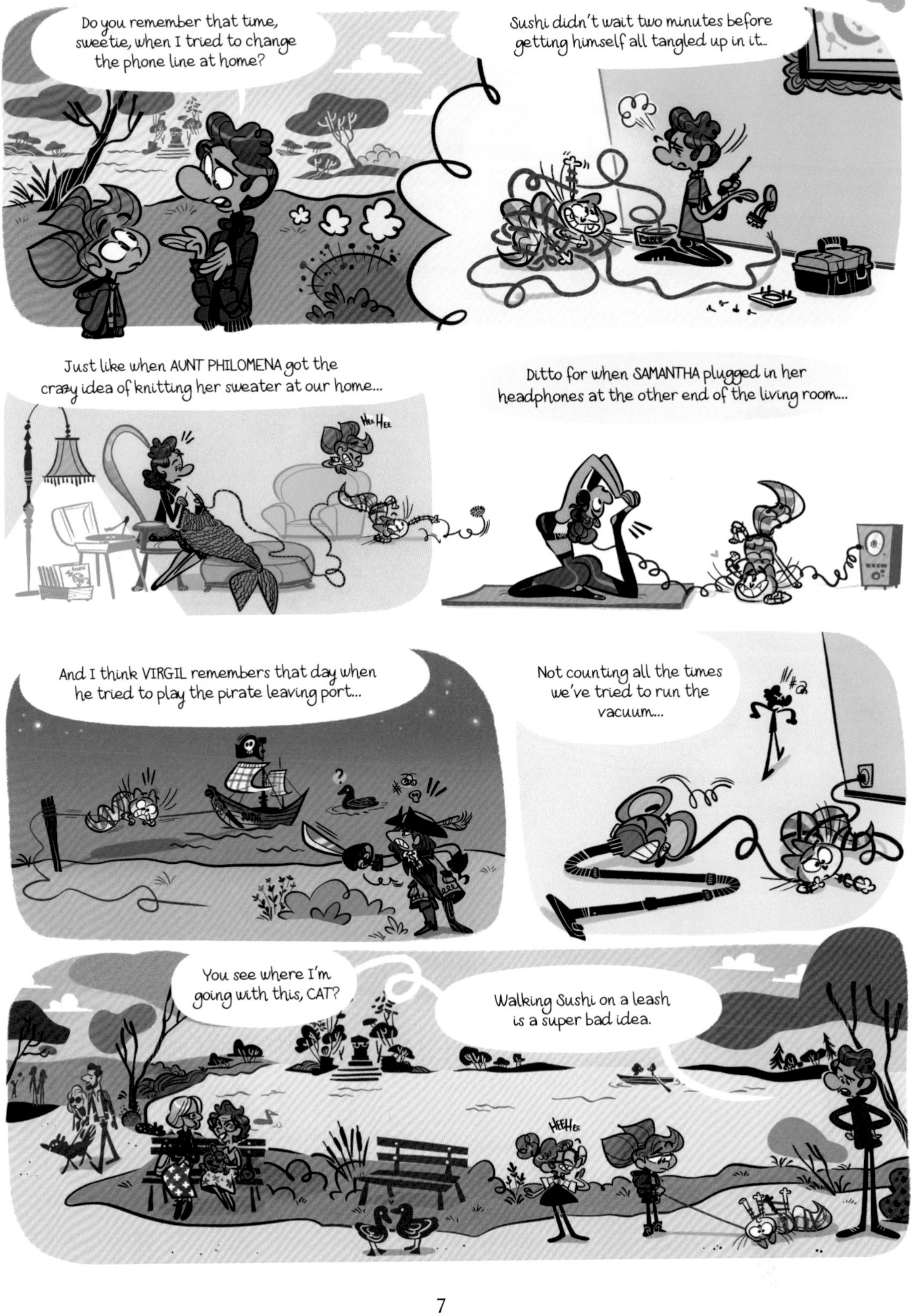
Do you remember that time, sweetie, when I tried to change the phone line at home?
Sushi didn't wait two minutes before getting himself all tangled up in it...
Just like when AUNT PHILOMENA got the crazy idea of knitting her sweater at our home...
HEE HEE
Ditto for when SAMANTHA plugged in her headphones at the other end of the living room...
And I think VIRGIL remembers that day when he tried to play the pirate leaving port...
SUSHI
Not counting all the times we've tried to run the vacuum...
You see where I'm going with this, CAT?
Walking Sushi on a leash is a super bad idea.
HEE HEE

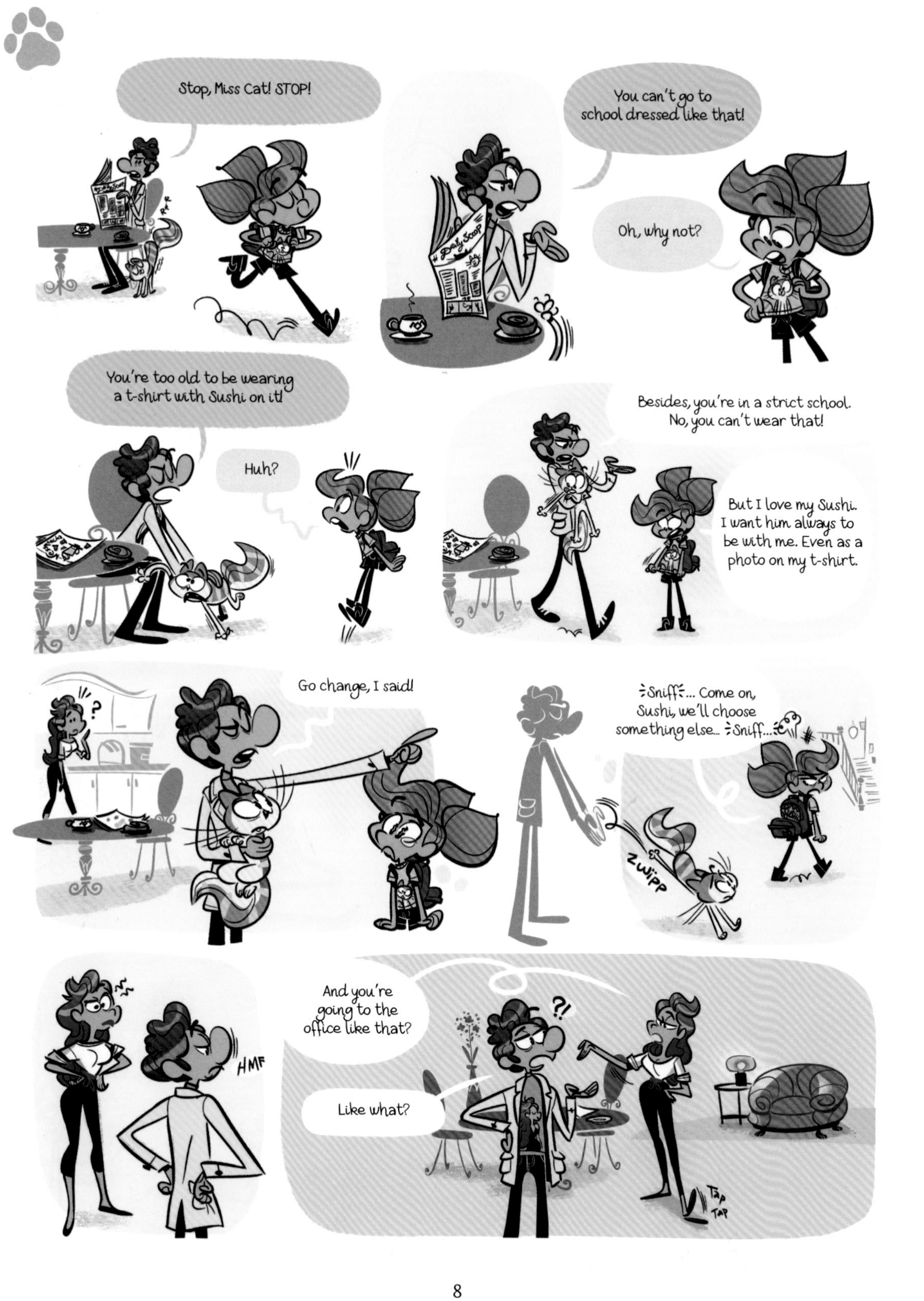
Stop, Miss Cat! STOP!
R-R
You can't go to school dressed like that!
Oh, why not?
You're too old to be wearing a t-shirt with Sushi on it!
Huh?
Besides, you're in a strict school. No, you can't wear that!
But I love my Sushi. I want him always to be with me. Even as a photo on my t-shirt.
Go change, I said!
Sniff... Come on, Sushi, we'll choose something else... Sniff...
ZWIPP
HMF
And you're going to the office like that?
?!
Like what?
TAP TAP

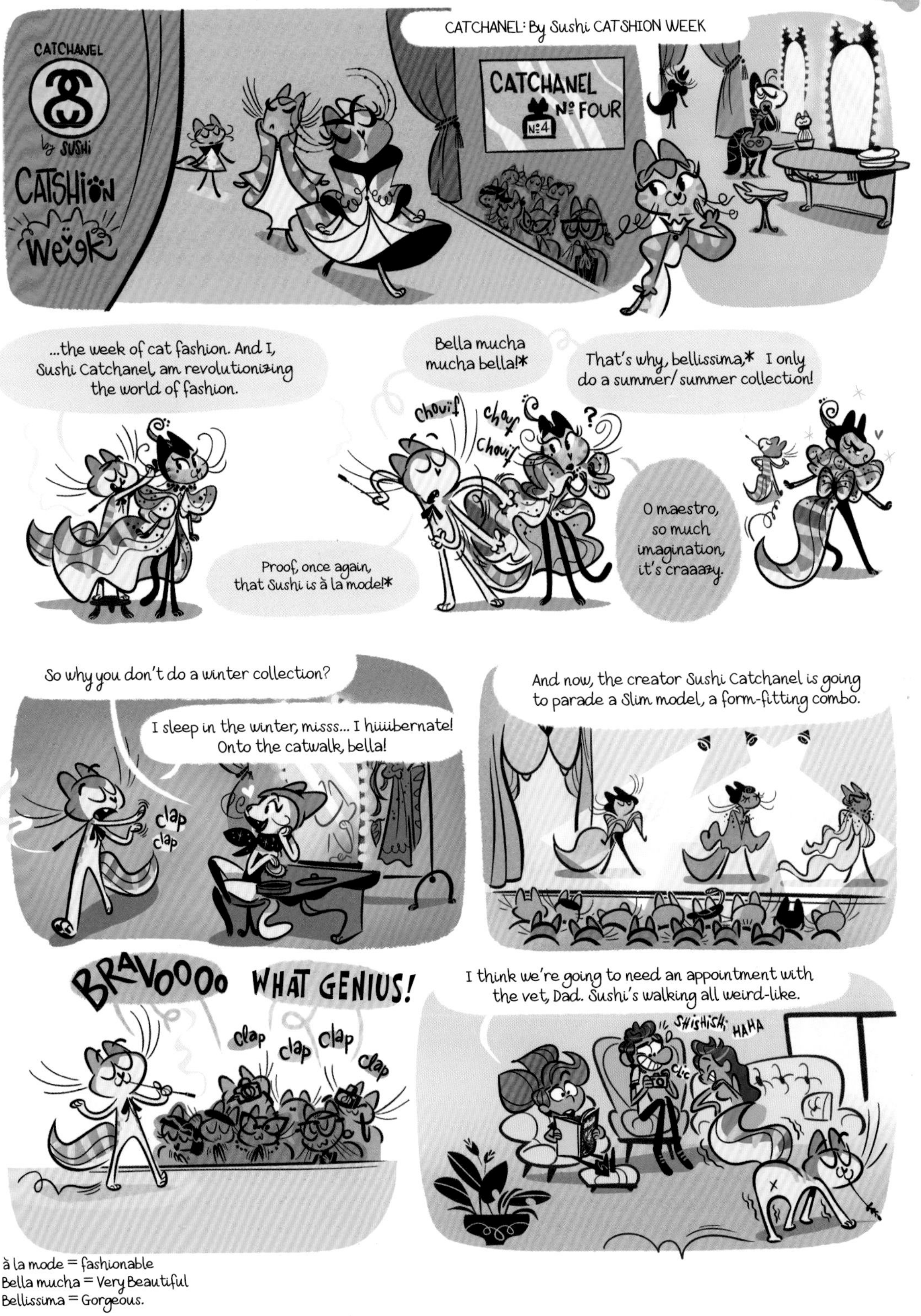
CATCHANEL: By Sushi CATSHION WEEK
CATCHANEL
by SUSHI
CATSHION WEEK
CATCHANEL Nº FOUR
Nº4
...the week of cat fashion. And I, Sushi Catchanel, am revolutionizing the world of fashion.
Proof, once again, that Sushi is à la mode!*
Bella mucha mucha bella!*
Chouif
Chouf
Chouif
That's why, bellissima,* I only do a summer/ summer collection!
O maestro, so much imagination, it's craaazy.
So why you don't do a winter collection?
I sleep in the winter, misss... I hiiiibernate! Onto the catwalk, bella!
clap
clap
And now, the creator Sushi Catchanel is going to parade a Slim model, a form-fitting combo.
BRAVOOOO WHAT GENIUS!
clap
clap
clap
clap
I think we're going to need an appointment with the vet, Dad. Sushi's walking all weird-like.
SHISHISHI HAHA
CLIC

* à la mode = fashionable
Bella mucha = Very Beautiful
Bellissima = Gorgeous.

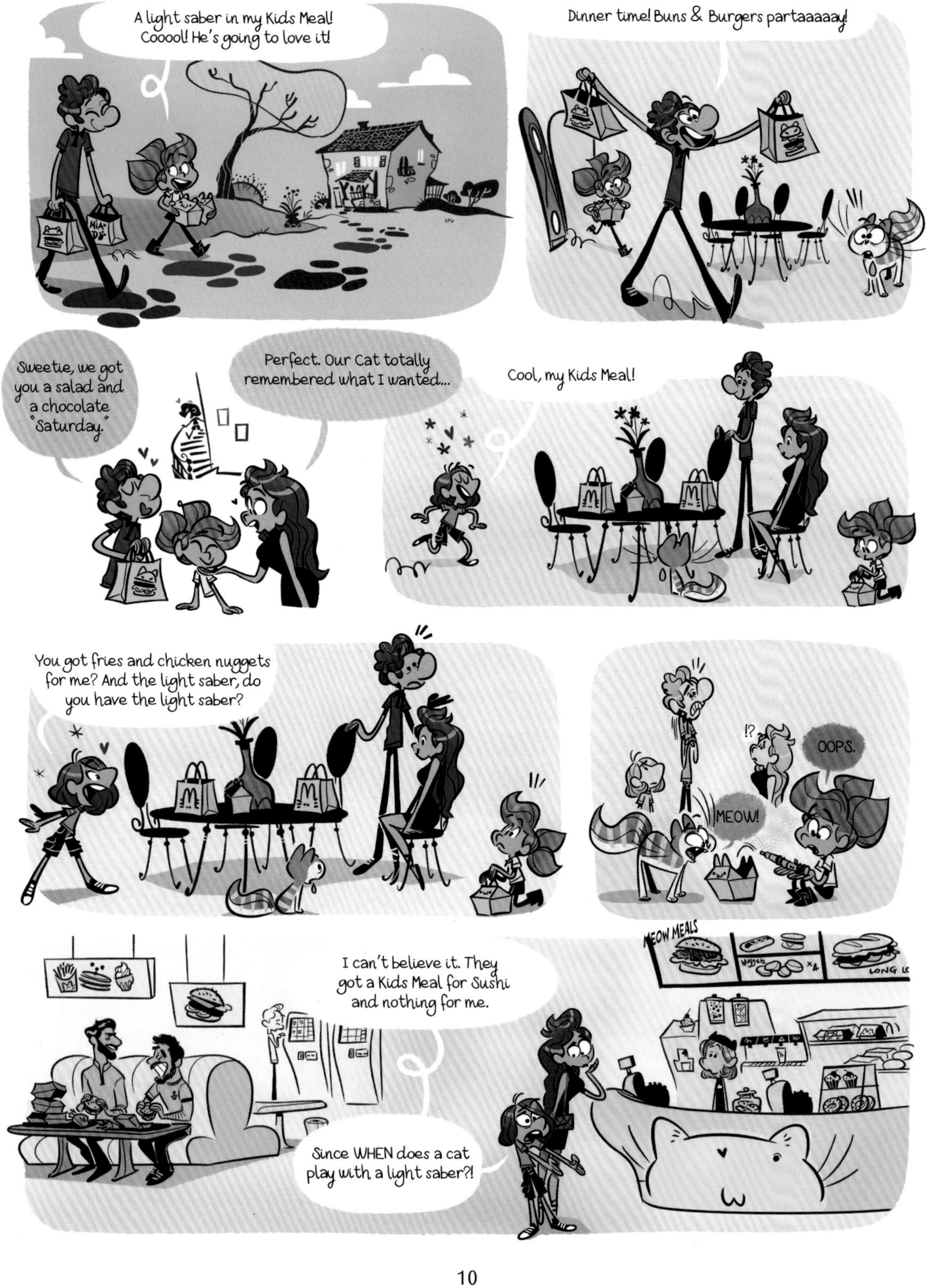
A light saber in my Kids Meal! Cooool! He's going to love it!
MIA
Dinner time! Buns & Burgers partaaaaay!
Sweetie, we got you a salad and a chocolate "Saturday."
Perfect. Our Cat totally remembered what I wanted...
Cool, my Kids Meal!
You got fries and chicken nuggets for me? And the light saber, do you have the light saber?
!?
OOPS.
MEOW!
MEOW MEALS
Nuggets
x4
I can't believe it. They got a Kids Meal for Sushi and nothing for me.
Since WHEN does a cat play with a light saber?!

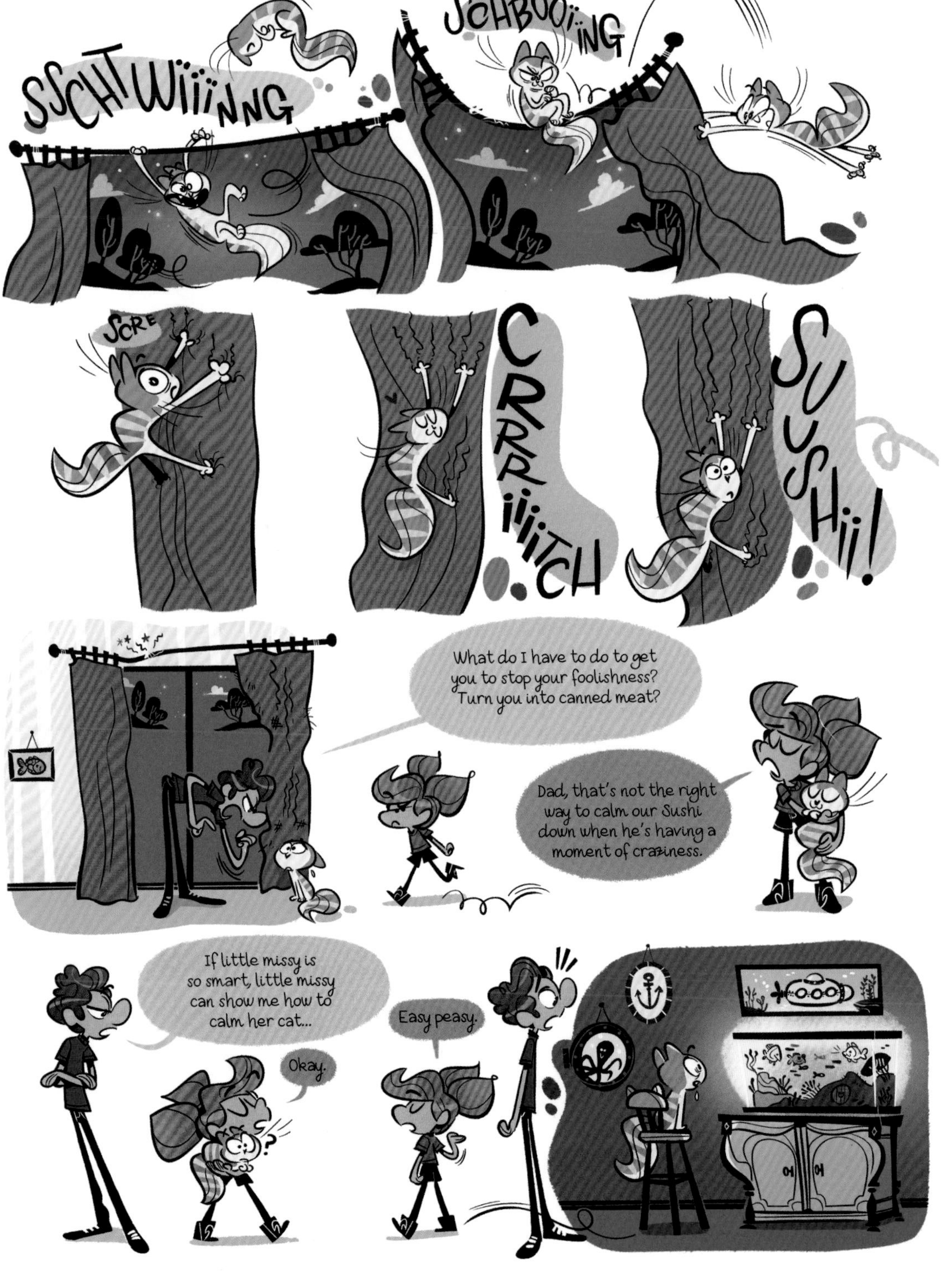
SSCHTWiiiiNNG
SCHBOOiiING
SCRE
CRRRiiiiTCH
SUSHii!
What do I have to do to get you to stop your foolishness? Turn you into canned meat?
Dad, that's not the right way to calm our Sushi down when he's having a moment of craziness.
If little missy is so smart, little missy can show me how to calm her cat...
Okay.
Easy peasy.

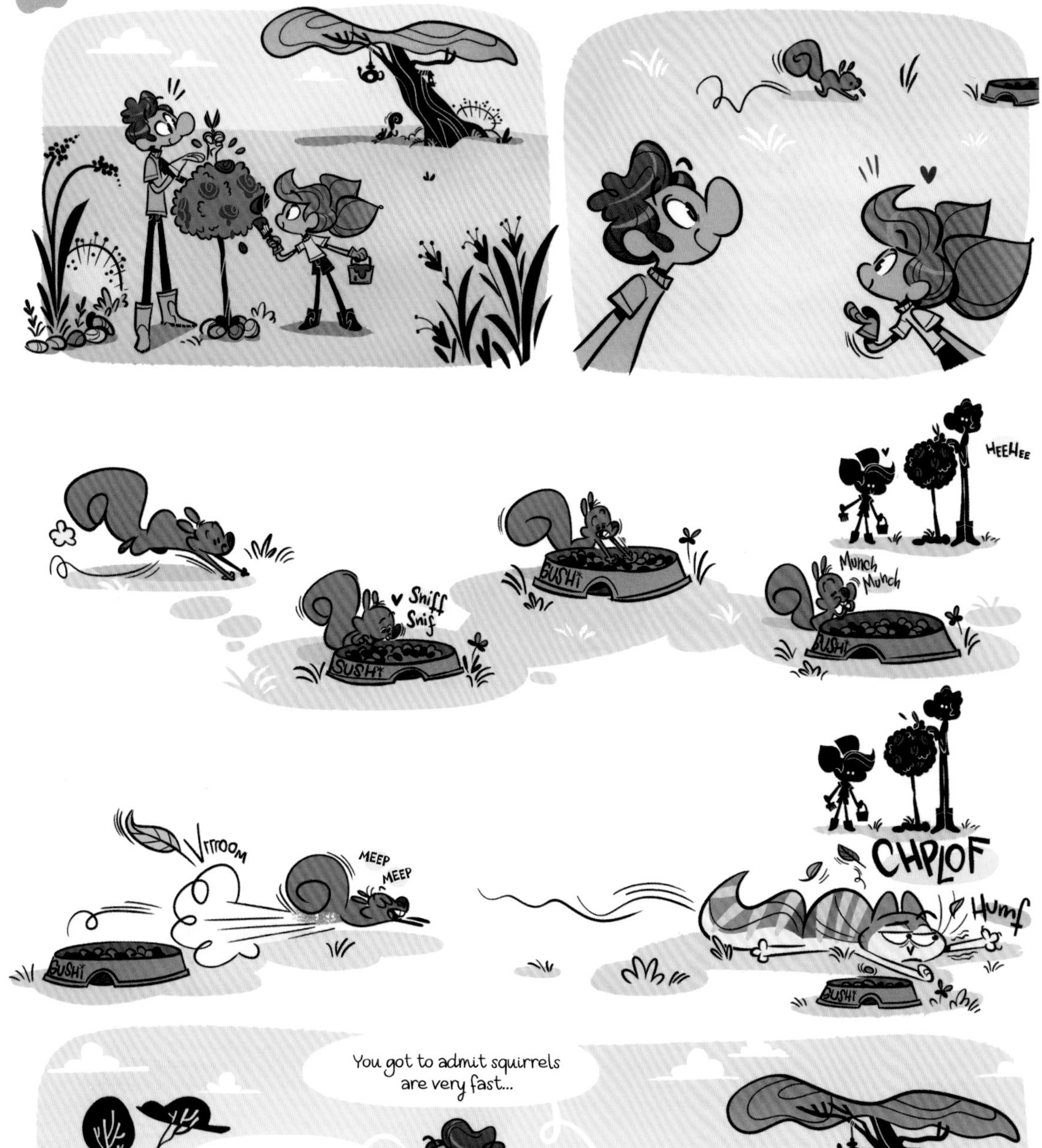

HEEHEE
Sniff
Snif
SUSHI
SUSHI
Munch
Munch
SUSHI
Vrrroom
MEEP
MEEP
SUSHI
CHPLOF
Humf
SUSHI
You got to admit squirrels are very fast...
It's mostly that Sushi is slow...
At least now we know it's not because of his kibble!

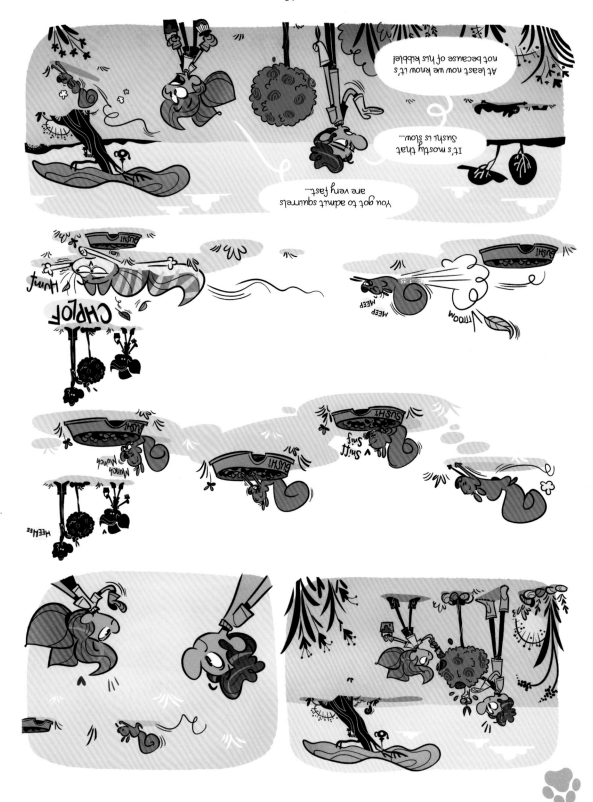

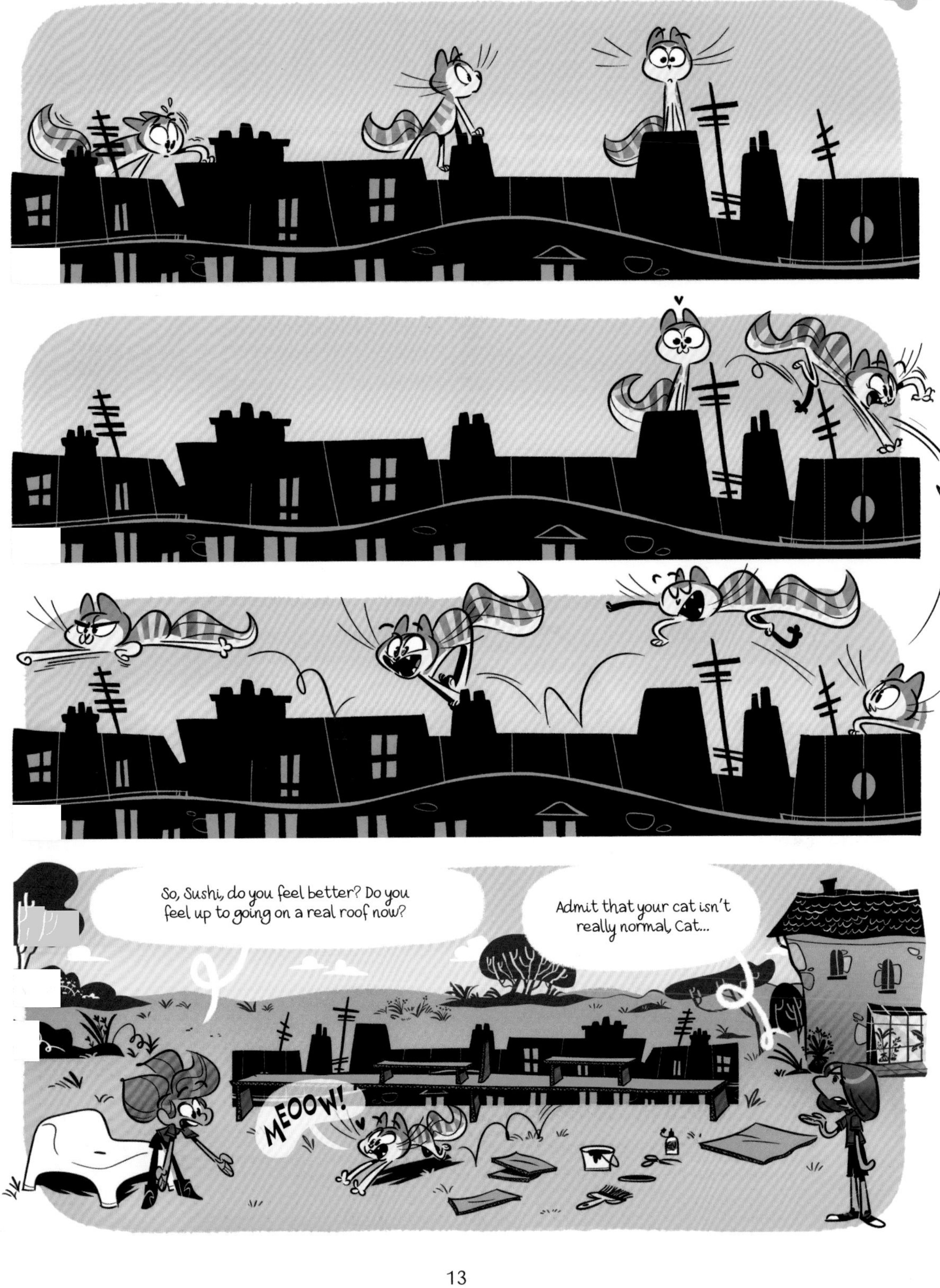
So, Sushi, do you feel better? Do you feel up to going on a real roof now?
Admit that your cat isn't really normal, Cat...
MEOOW!

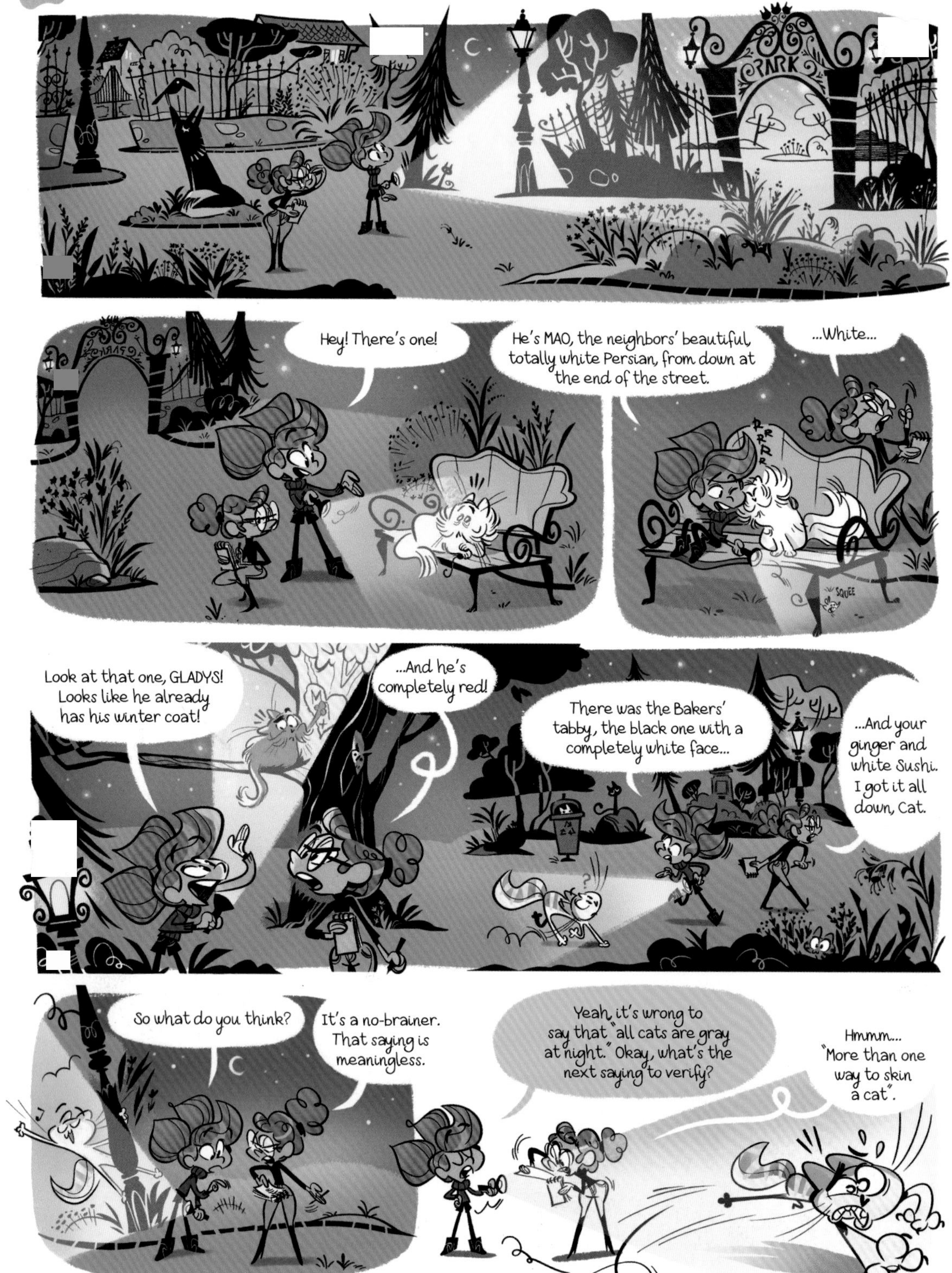
PARK
Hey! There's one!
He's MAO, the neighbors' beautiful, totally white Persian, from down at the end of the street.
...White...
RRRR
SQUEE
Look at that one, GLADYS! Looks like he already has his winter coat!
...And he's completely red!
There was the Bakers' tabby, the black one with a completely white face...
...And your ginger and white Sushi. I got it all down, Cat.
So what do you think?
It's a no-brainer. That saying is meaningless.
Yeah, it's wrong to say that "all cats are gray at night." Okay, what's the next saying to verify?
Hmmm... "More than one way to skin a cat".

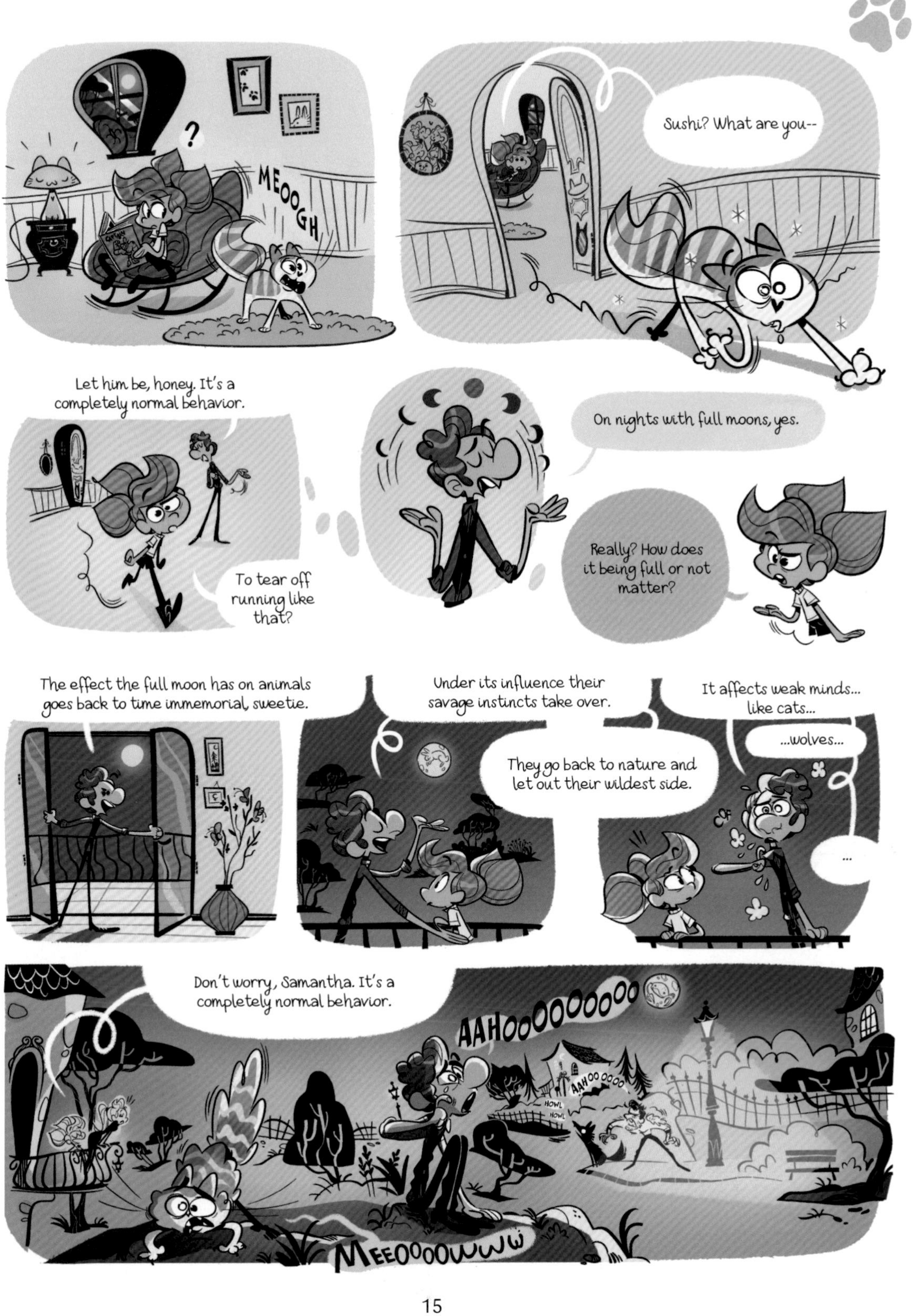
?
MEOOGH
Sushi? What are you--
Let him be, honey. It's a completely normal behavior.
To tear off running like that?
On nights with full moons, yes.
Really? How does it being full or not matter?
The effect the full moon has on animals goes back to time immemorial, sweetie.
Under its influence their savage instincts take over.
They go back to nature and let out their wildest side.
It affects weak minds... like cats...
...wolves...
...
Don't worry, Samantha. It's a completely normal behavior.
AAHOOOOOOOOOO
AAHOO OOOO
HOWL
HOWL
MEEOOOOWWW

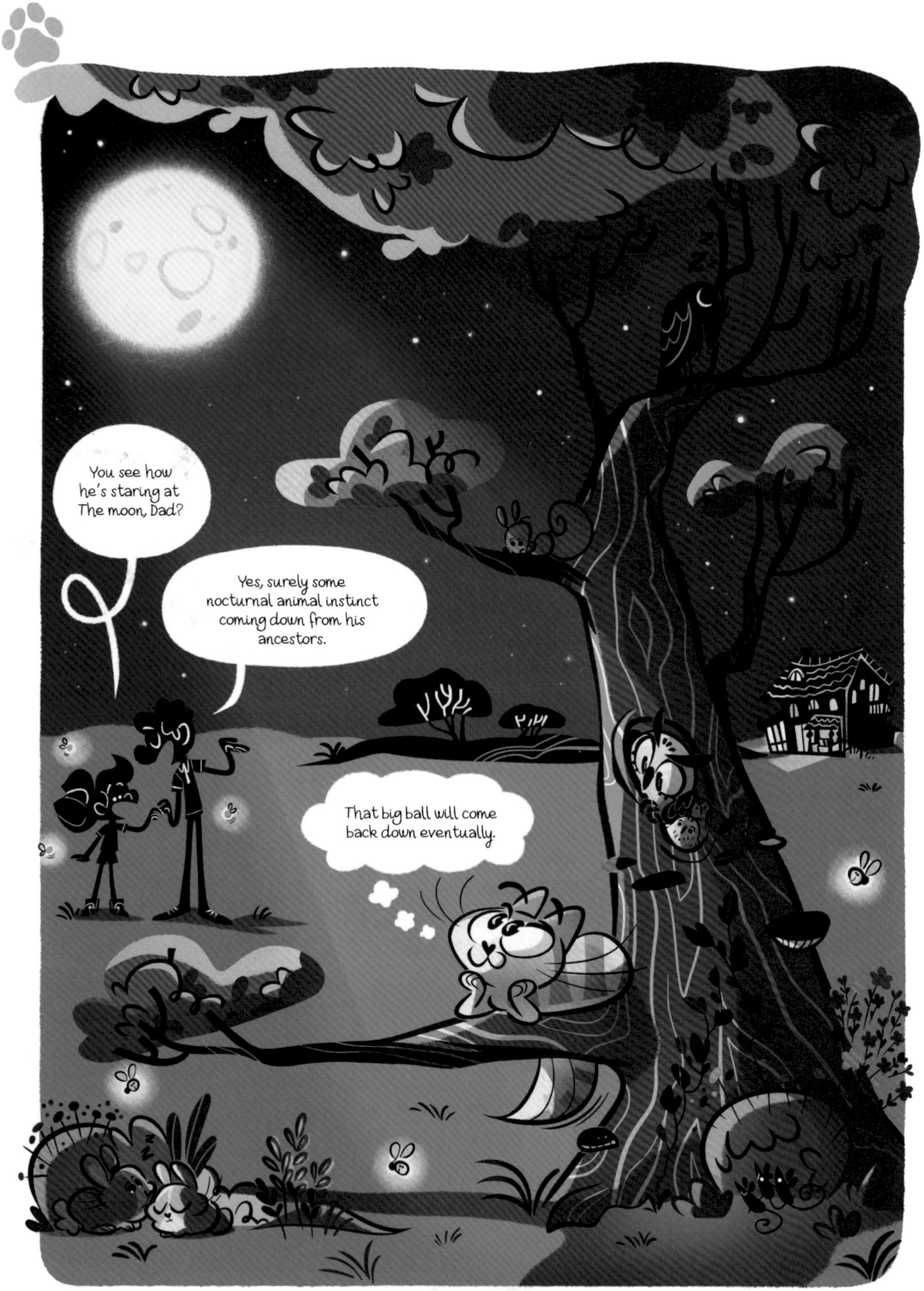
You see how he's staring at The moon, Dad?
Yes, surely some nocturnal animal instinct coming down from his ancestors.
That big ball will come back down eventually.

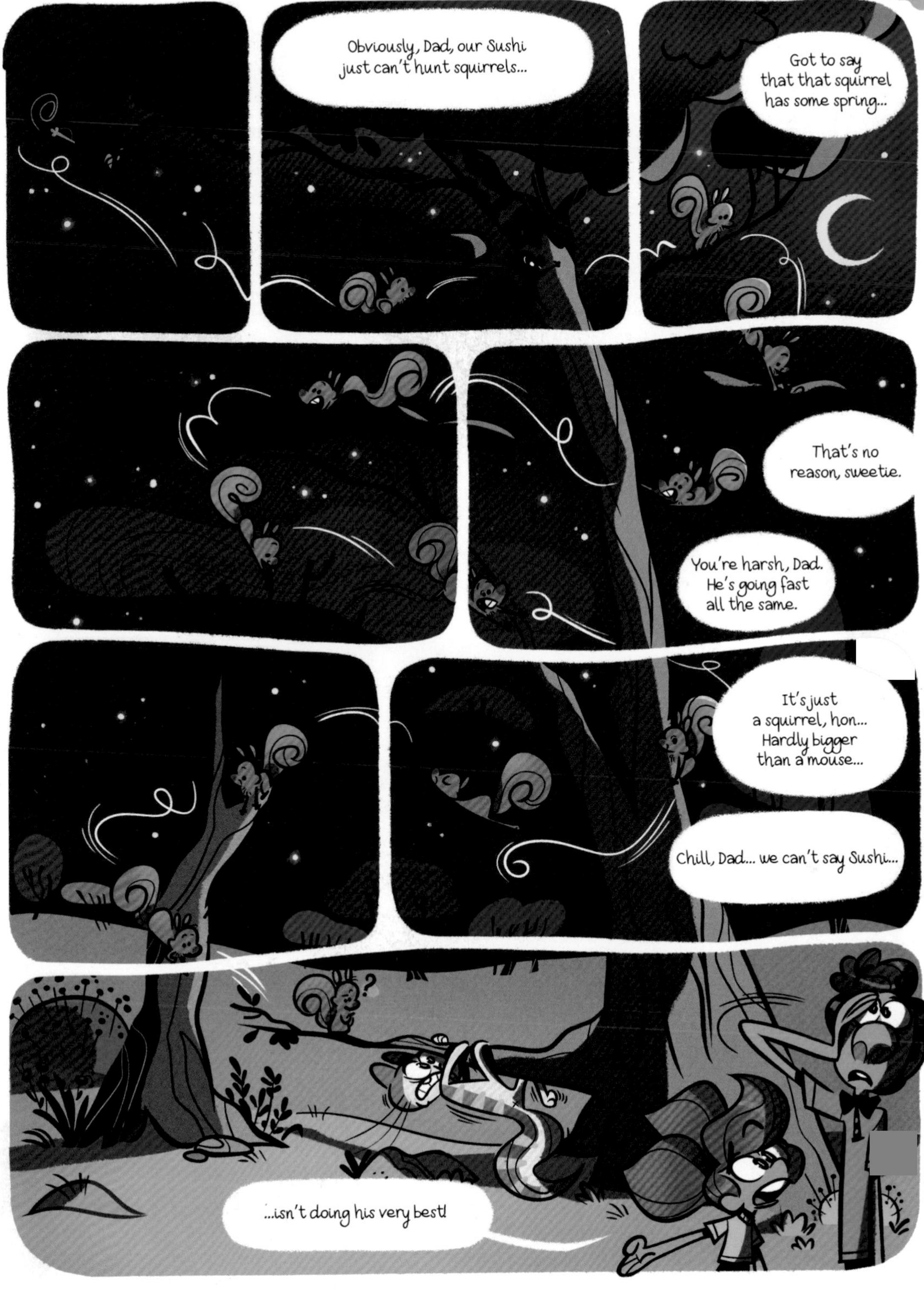
Obviously, Dad, our Sushi just can't hunt squirrels...
Got to say that that squirrel has some spring...
That's no reason, sweetie.
You're harsh, Dad. He's going fast all the same.
It's just a squirrel, hon... Hardly bigger than a mouse...
Chill, Dad... we can't say Sushi...
...isn't doing his very best!

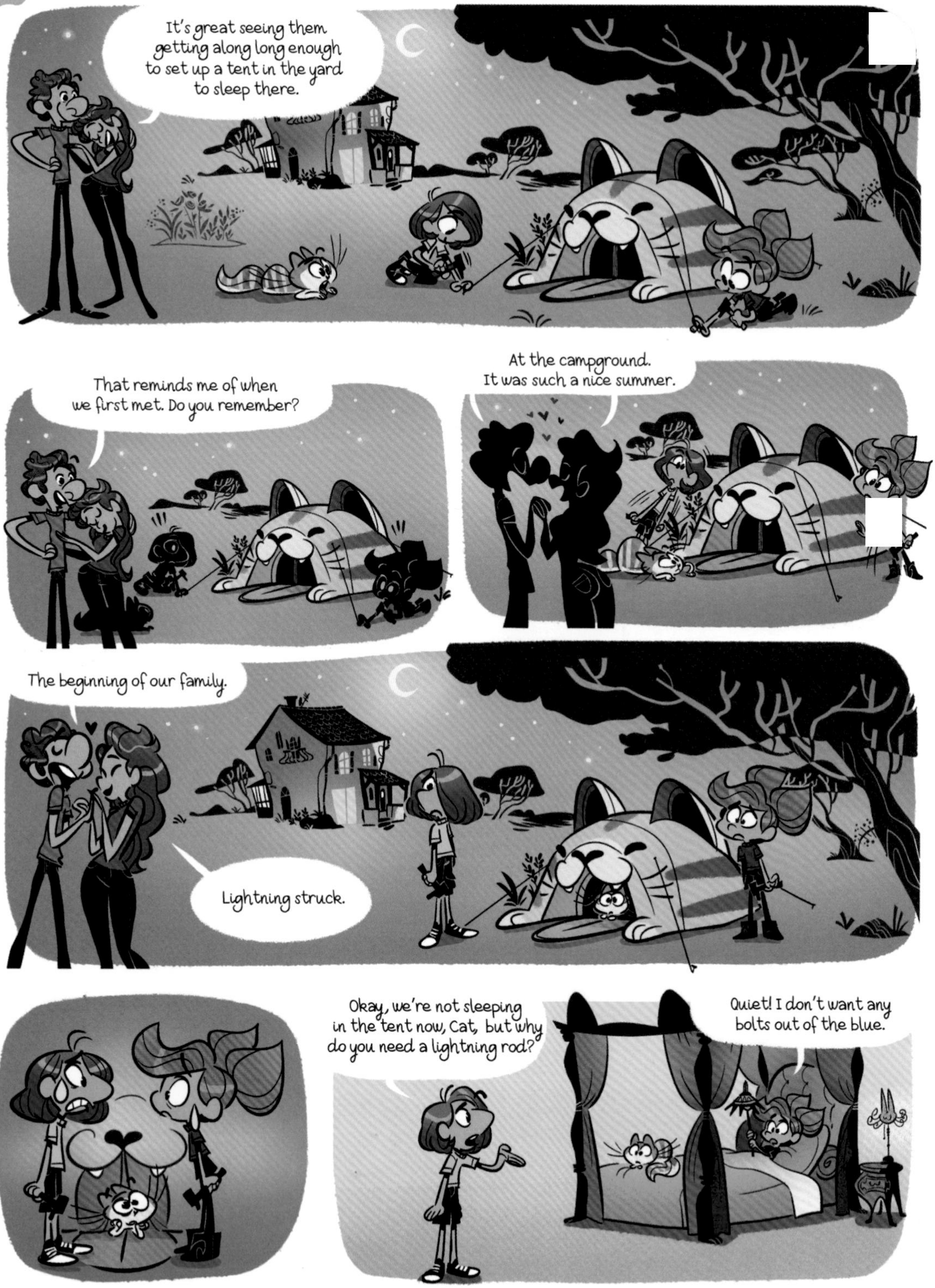
It's great seeing them getting along long enough to set up a tent in the yard to sleep there.
That reminds me of when we first met. Do you remember?
At the campground. It was such a nice summer.
The beginning of our family.
Lightning struck.
Okay, we're not sleeping in the tent now, Cat, but why do you need a lightning rod?
Quiet! I don't want any bolts out of the blue.

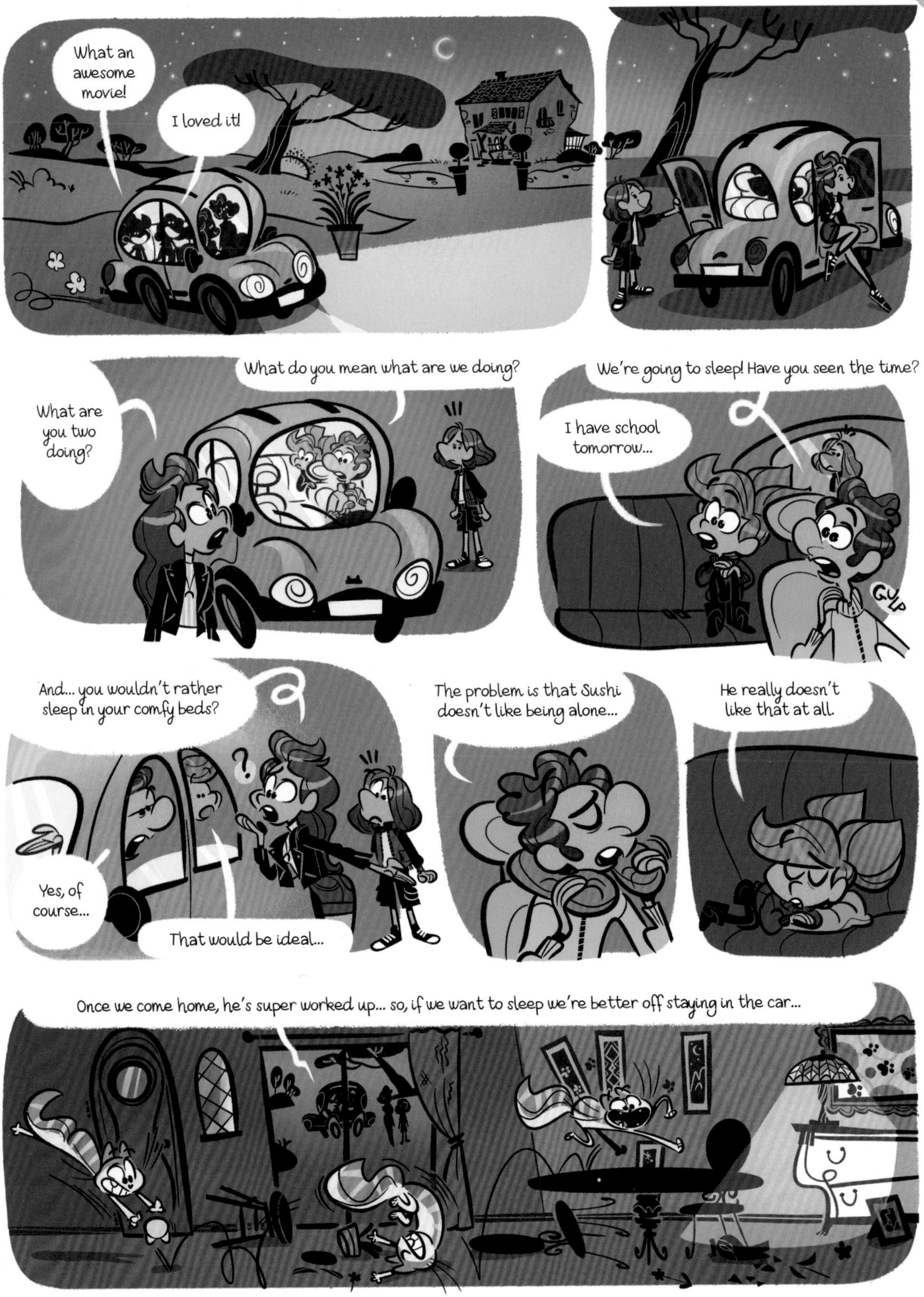
What an awesome movie!
I loved it!
What are you two doing?
What do you mean what are we doing?
We're going to sleep! Have you seen the time?
I have school tomorrow...
GULP
And... you wouldn't rather sleep in your comfy beds?
Yes, of course...
That would be ideal...
The problem is that Sushi doesn't like being alone...
He really doesn't like that at all.
Once we come home, he's super worked up... so, if we want to sleep we're better off staying in the car...

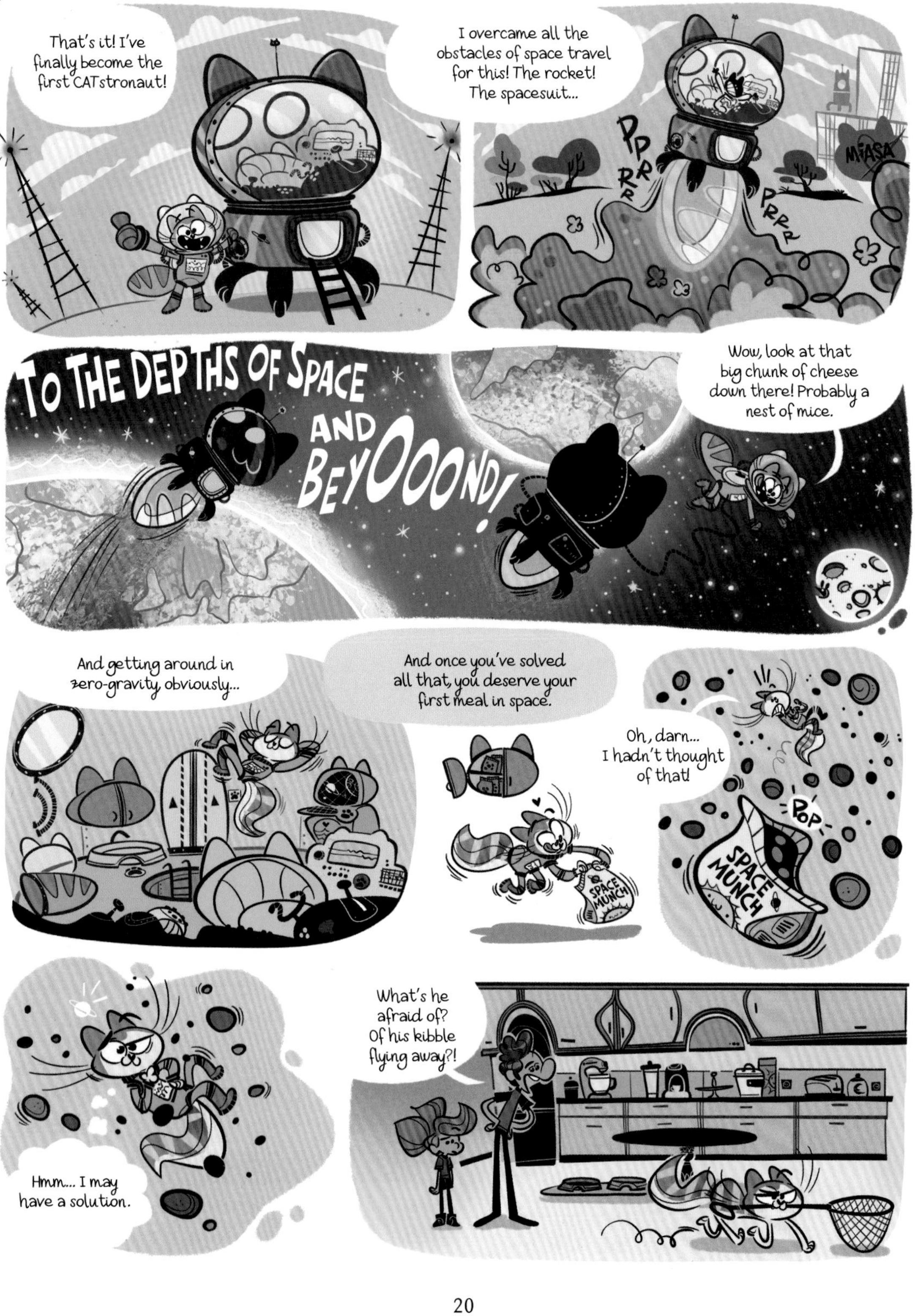
That's it! I've finally become the first CATstronaut!
I overcame all the obstacles of space travel for this! The rocket! The spacesuit...
PPRRR
PRRRR
MIASA
TO THE DEPTHS OF SPACE AND BEYOOOND!
Wow, look at that big chunk of cheese down there! Probably a nest of mice.
And getting around in zero-gravity, obviously...
And once you've solved all that, you deserve your first meal in space.
Oh, darn... I hadn't thought of that!
POP
SPACE MUNCH
Hmm... I may have a solution.
What's he afraid of? Of his kibble flying away?!

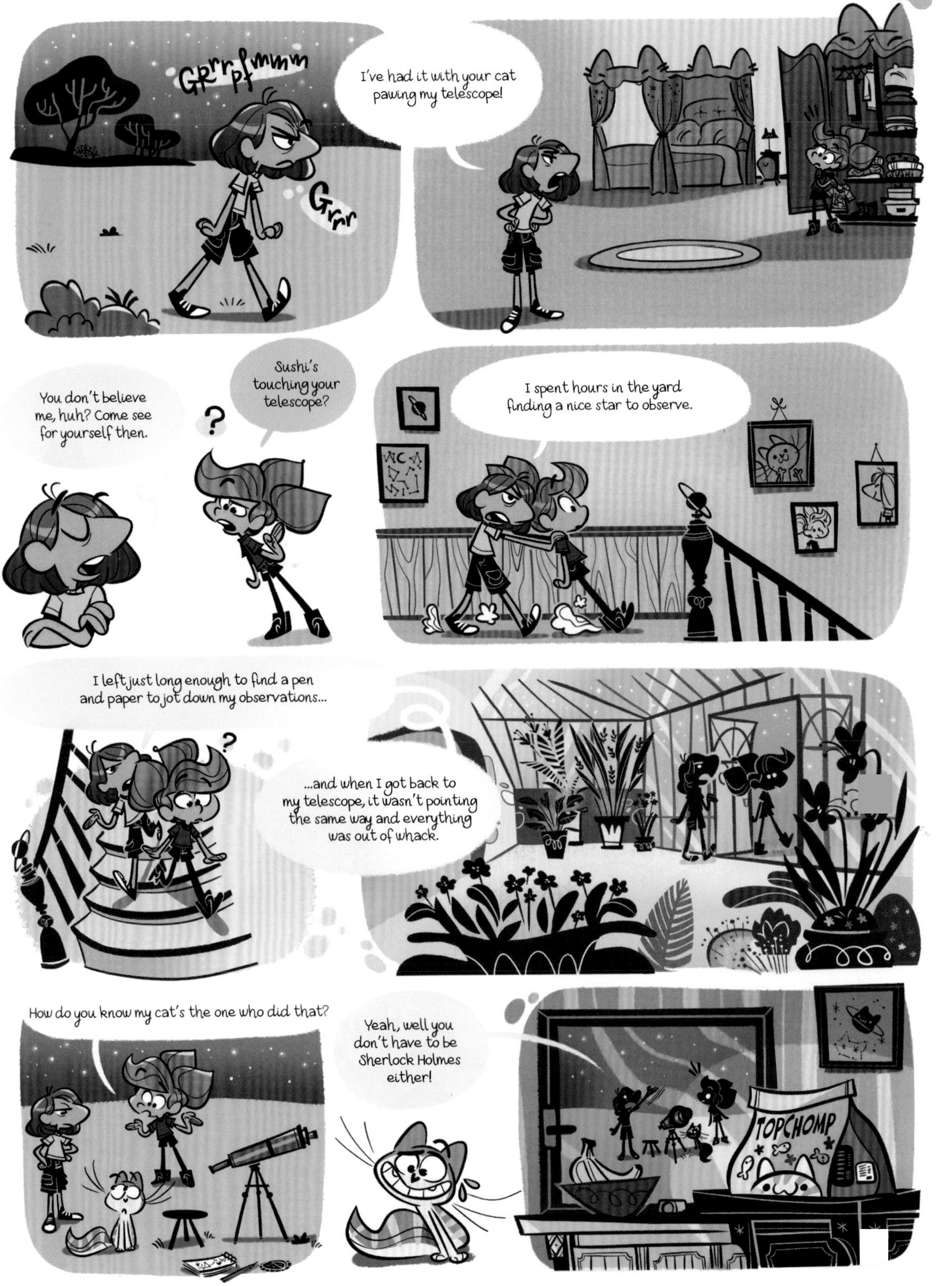
Grrrpfmmm
Grrr
I've had it with your cat pawing my telescope!
You don't believe me, huh? Come see for yourself then.
?
Sushi's touching your telescope?
I spent hours in the yard finding a nice star to observe.
I left just long enough to find a pen and paper to jot down my observations...
?
...and when I got back to my telescope, it wasn't pointing the same way and everything was out of whack.
How do you know my cat's the one who did that?
Yeah, well you don't have to be Sherlock Holmes either!
TOPCHOMP

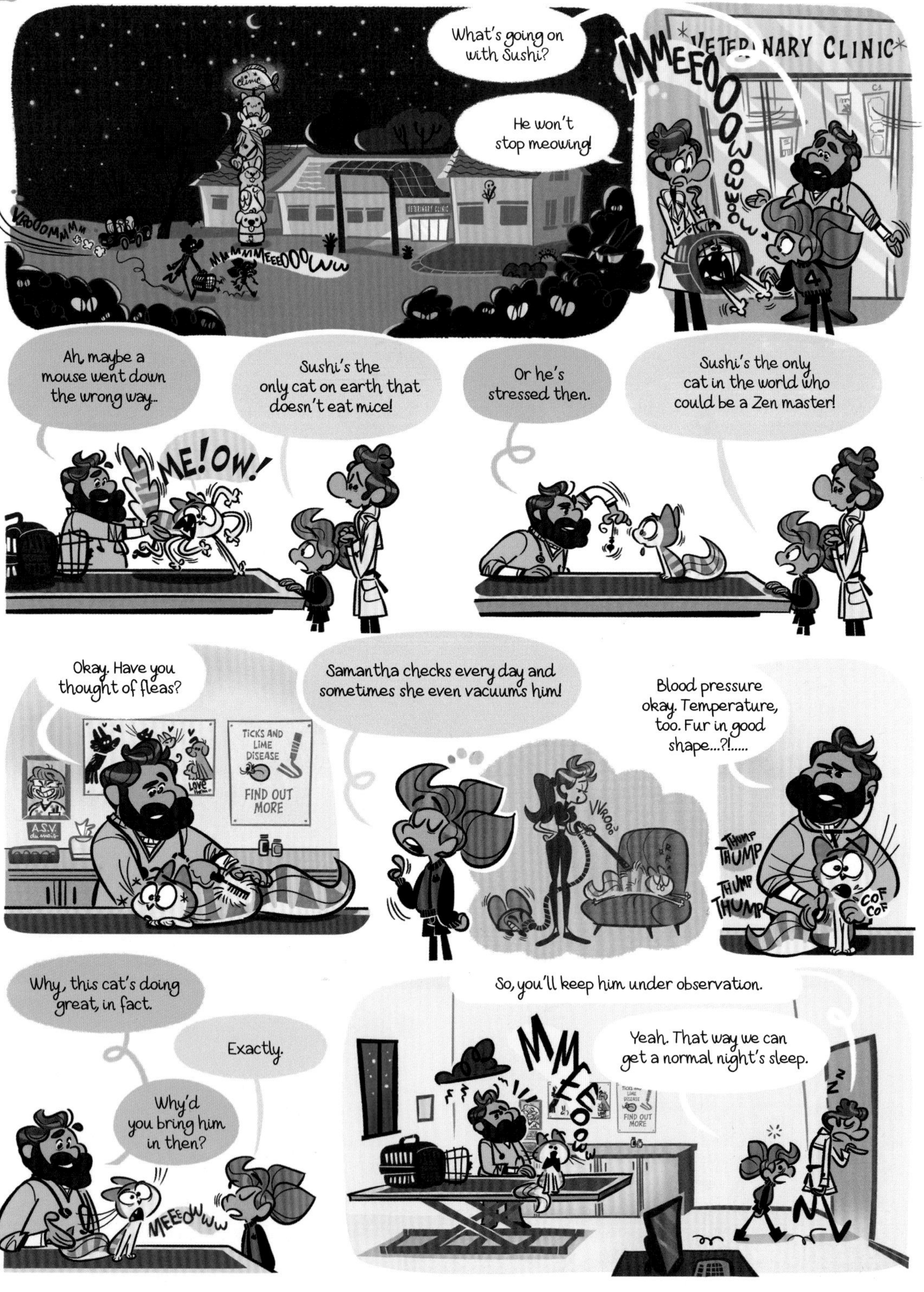
VROOOMMMM
MMMMMMEEEOOOWW
What's going on with Sushi?
He won't stop meowing!
VETERINARY CLINIC
MMEEOOOOOWOWWOOOW
Ah, maybe a mouse went down the wrong way...
Sushi's the only cat on earth that doesn't eat mice!
ME!OW!
Or he's stressed then.
Sushi's the only cat in the world who could be a Zen master!
Okay. Have you thought of fleas?
TICKS AND LIME DISEASE
FIND OUT MORE
Samantha checks every day and sometimes she even vacuums him!
VVROOO
Blood pressure okay. Temperature, too. Fur in good shape...?!.....
THUMP THUMP
THUMP THUMP
COF COF
Why, this cat's doing great, in fact.
Exactly.
Why'd you bring him in then?
MEEEOWWW
So, you'll keep him under observation.
Yeah. That way we can get a normal night's sleep.
MMEEOOW

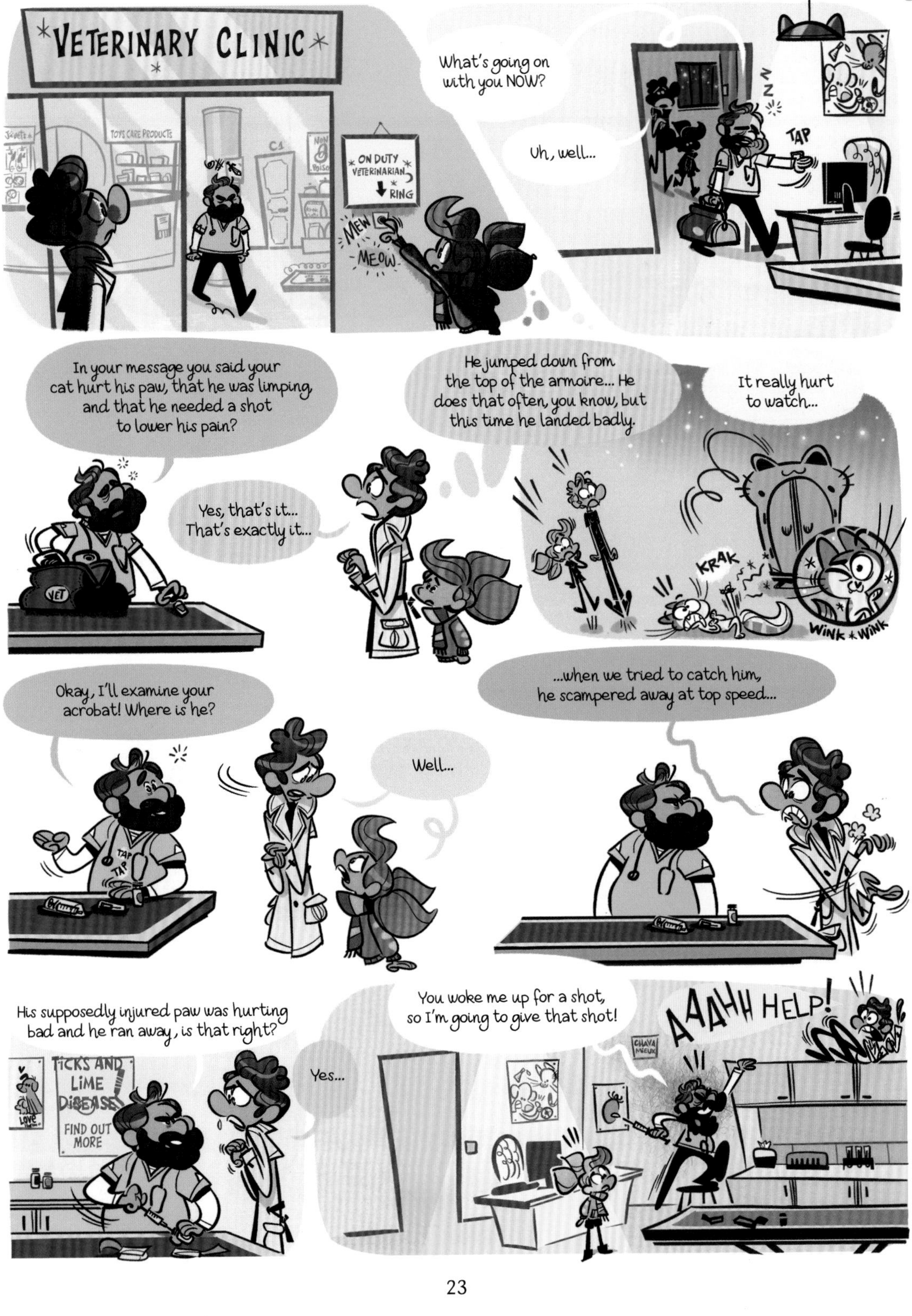
VETERINARY CLINIC
TOYS CARE PRODUCTS
ON DUTY VETERINARIAN RING
MEW
MEOW
What's going on with you NOW?
Uh, well...
TAP
In your message you said your cat hurt his paw, that he was limping and that he needed a shot to lower his pain?
Yes, that's it... That's exactly it...
VET
He jumped down from the top of the armoire... He does that often, you know, but this time he landed badly.
It really hurt to watch...
KRAK
WINK WINK
Okay, I'll examine your acrobat! Where is he?
TAP TAP
Well...
...when we tried to catch him, he scampered away at top speed...
His supposedly injured paw was hurting bad and he ran away, is that right?
TICKS AND LIME DISEASE FIND OUT MORE
LOVE
Yes...
You woke me up for a shot, so I'm going to give that shot!
AAAHH HELP!

Tonight are you interested in spying on our parents in their bedroom?
Coooool! How do we do it?
We'll put a GoPro camera on Sushi and send him to look through their window... You think he can do it?
Of course, he's the greatest spy cat in my secret service.
Let's go, kitty! Go spy on our parents!
MEW! MEW!
You can't see much...
That's normal, Cat. It's nighttime.
Yeah, but how will we spy on our parents if we can't see anything?
Well, I don't have just any GoPro. I have the top model!
Oh, yeah. And what does the top model have?
A flash...
Pffff... now we're the ones who are going to see the big white light.

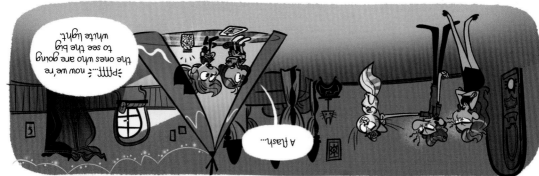

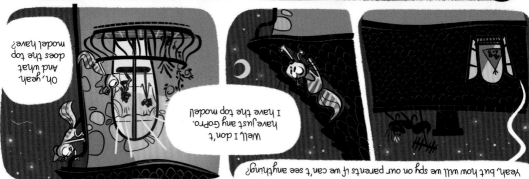

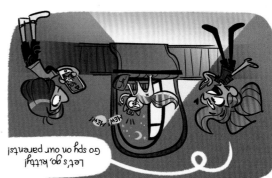

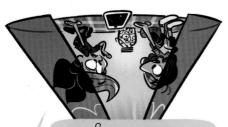

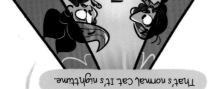

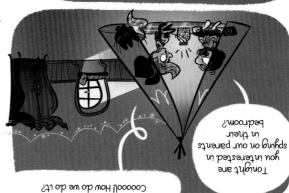

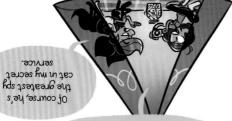

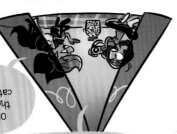

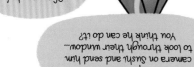

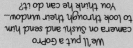

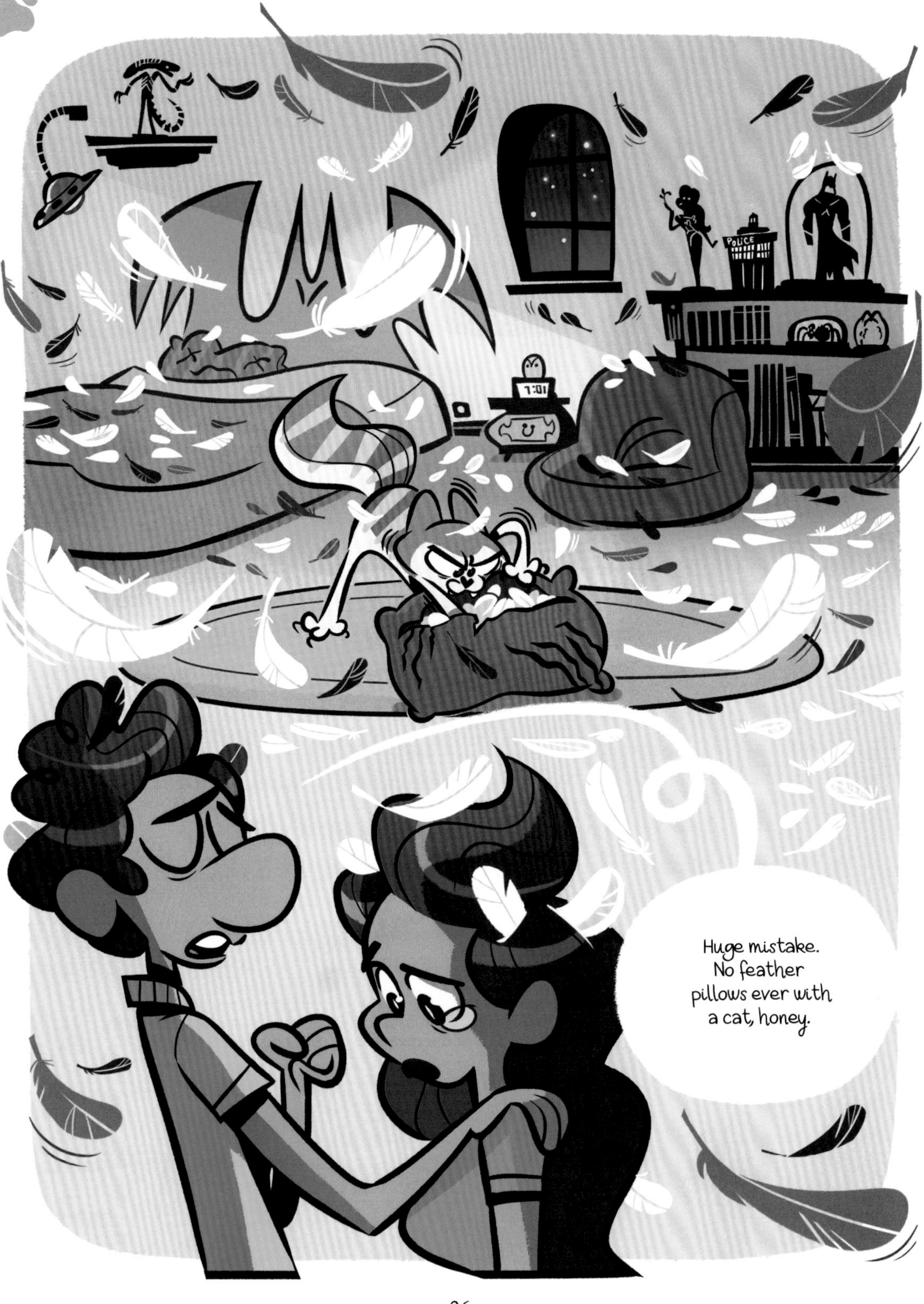
POLICE
7:01
Huge mistake. No feather pillows ever with a cat, honey.

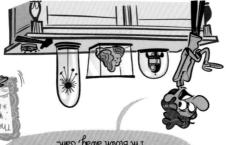

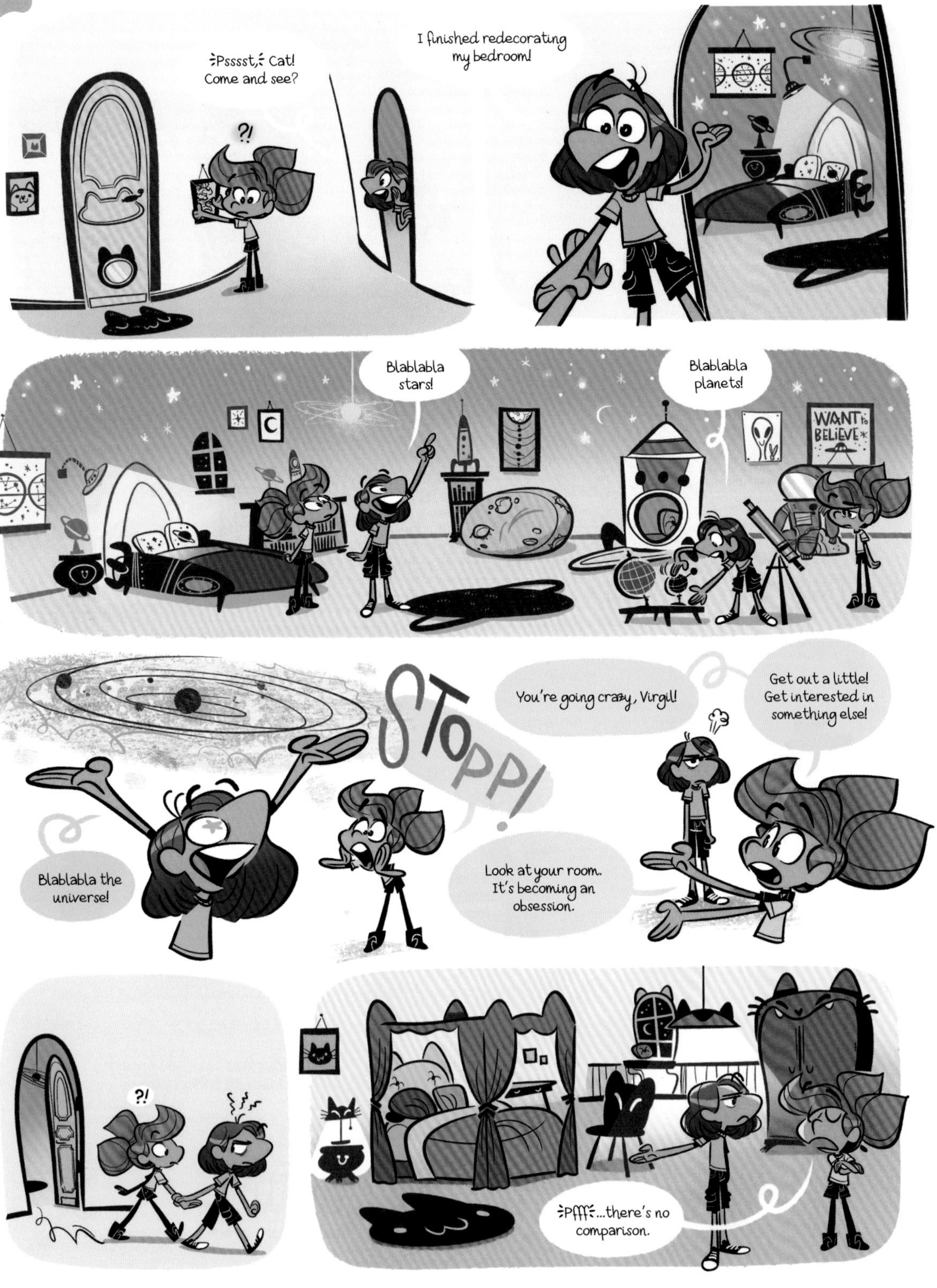
Psssst, Cat! Come and see?
?!
I finished redecorating my bedroom!
Blablabla stars!
Blablabla planets!
WANT to BELIEVE
STOPP!
You're going crazy, Virgil!
Get out a little! Get interested in something else!
Blablabla the universe!
Look at your room. It's becoming an obsession.
?!
Pfff...there's no comparison.

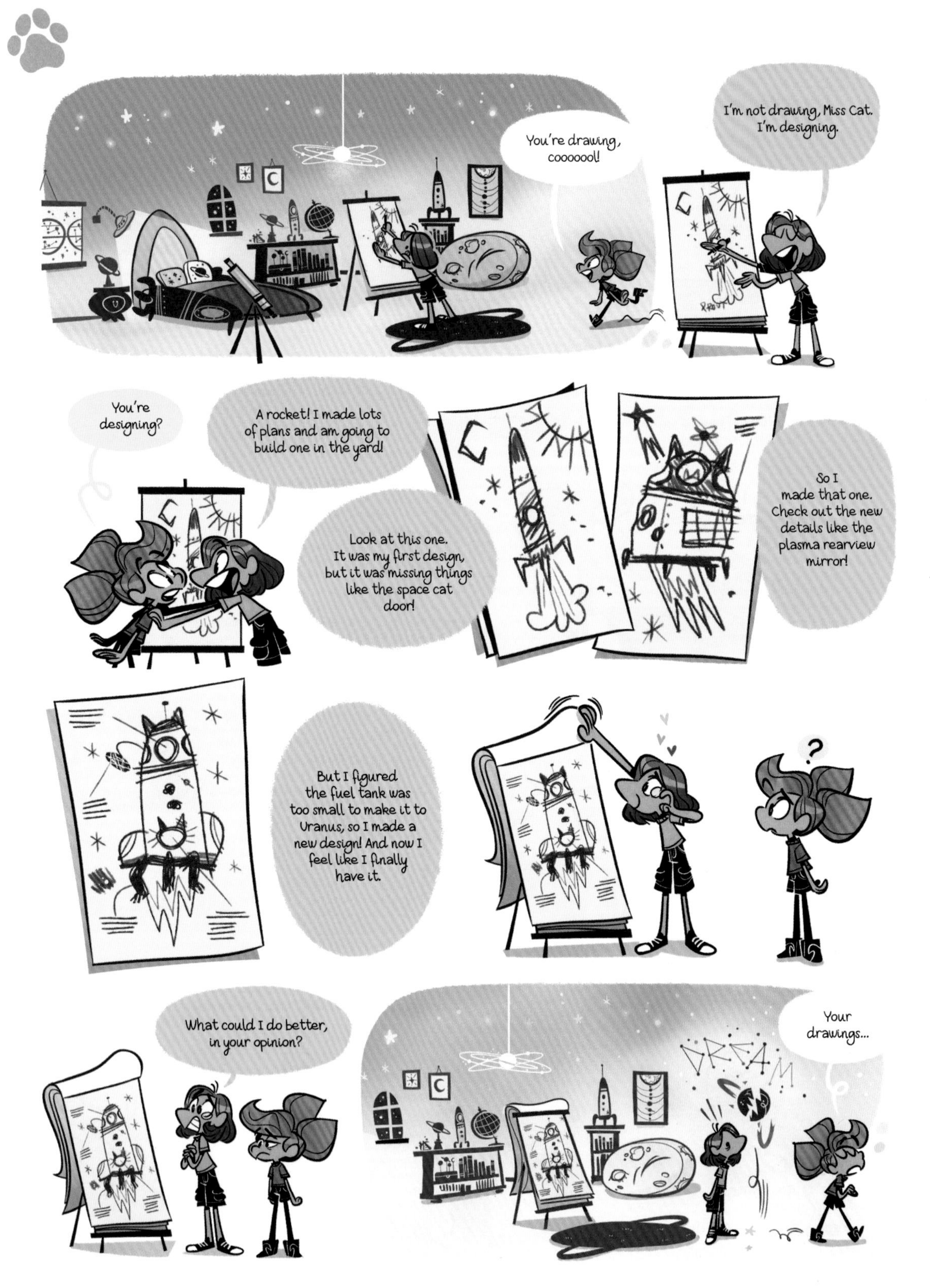
You're drawing, coooooool!
I'm not drawing, Miss Cat. I'm designing.
You're designing?
A rocket! I made lots of plans and am going to build one in the yard!
Look at this one. It was my first design, but it was missing things like the space cat door!
So I made that one. Check out the new details like the plasma rearview mirror!
But I figured the fuel tank was too small to make it to Uranus, so I made a new design! And now I feel like I finally have it.
?
What could I do better, in your opinion?
Your drawings...
DREAM

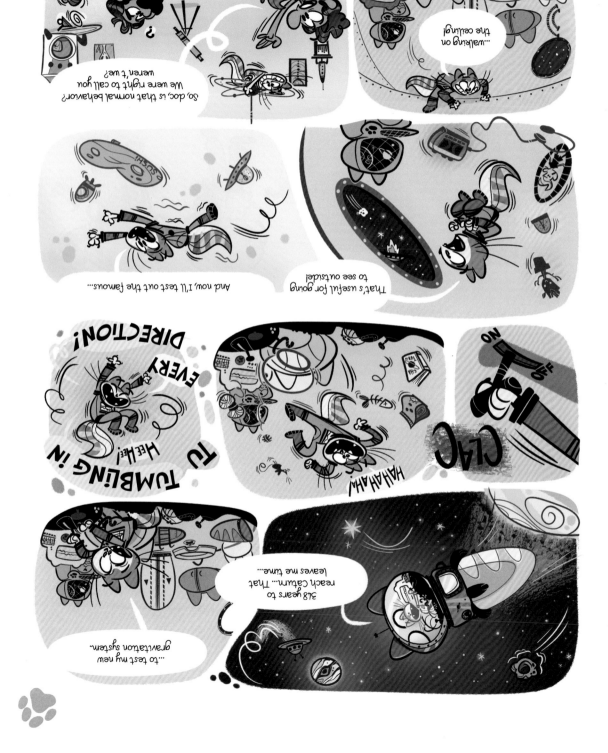

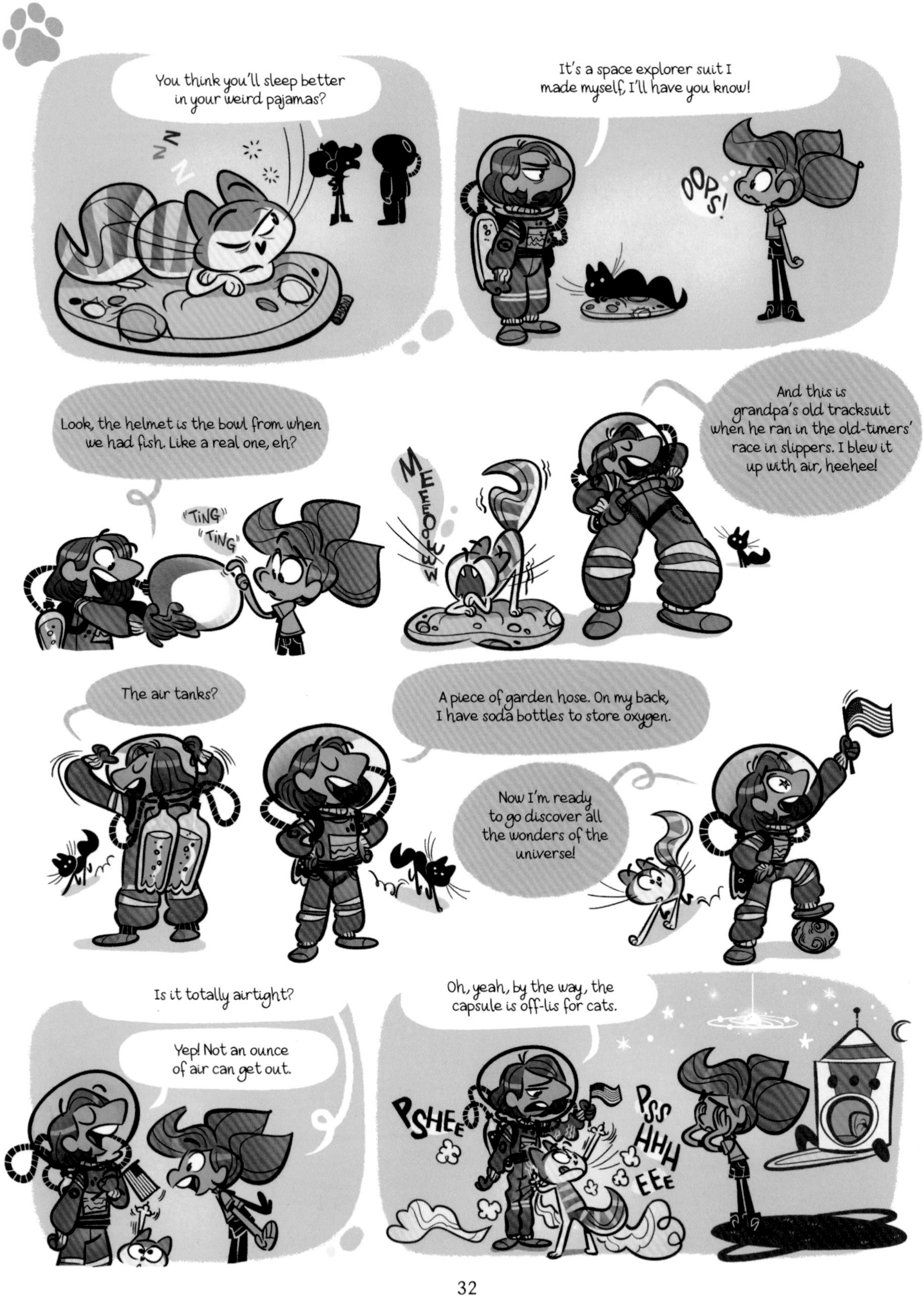

You think you'll sleep better in your weird pajamas?

It's a space explorer suit I made myself, I'll have you know!

OOPS!

Look, the helmet is the bowl from when we had fish. Like a real one, eh?

"TING" "TING"

MEEEOOUWW

And this is grandpa's old tracksuit when he ran in the old-timers' race in slippers. I blew it up with air, heehee!

The air tanks?

A piece of garden hose. On my back, I have soda bottles to store oxygen.

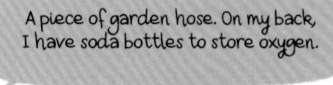

Now I'm ready to go discover all the wonders of the universe!

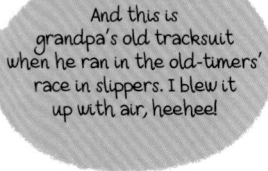

Is it totally airtight?

Yep! Not an ounce of air can get out.

Oh, yeah, by the way, the capsule is off-lis for cats.

PSHEE

PSSHHHEEE

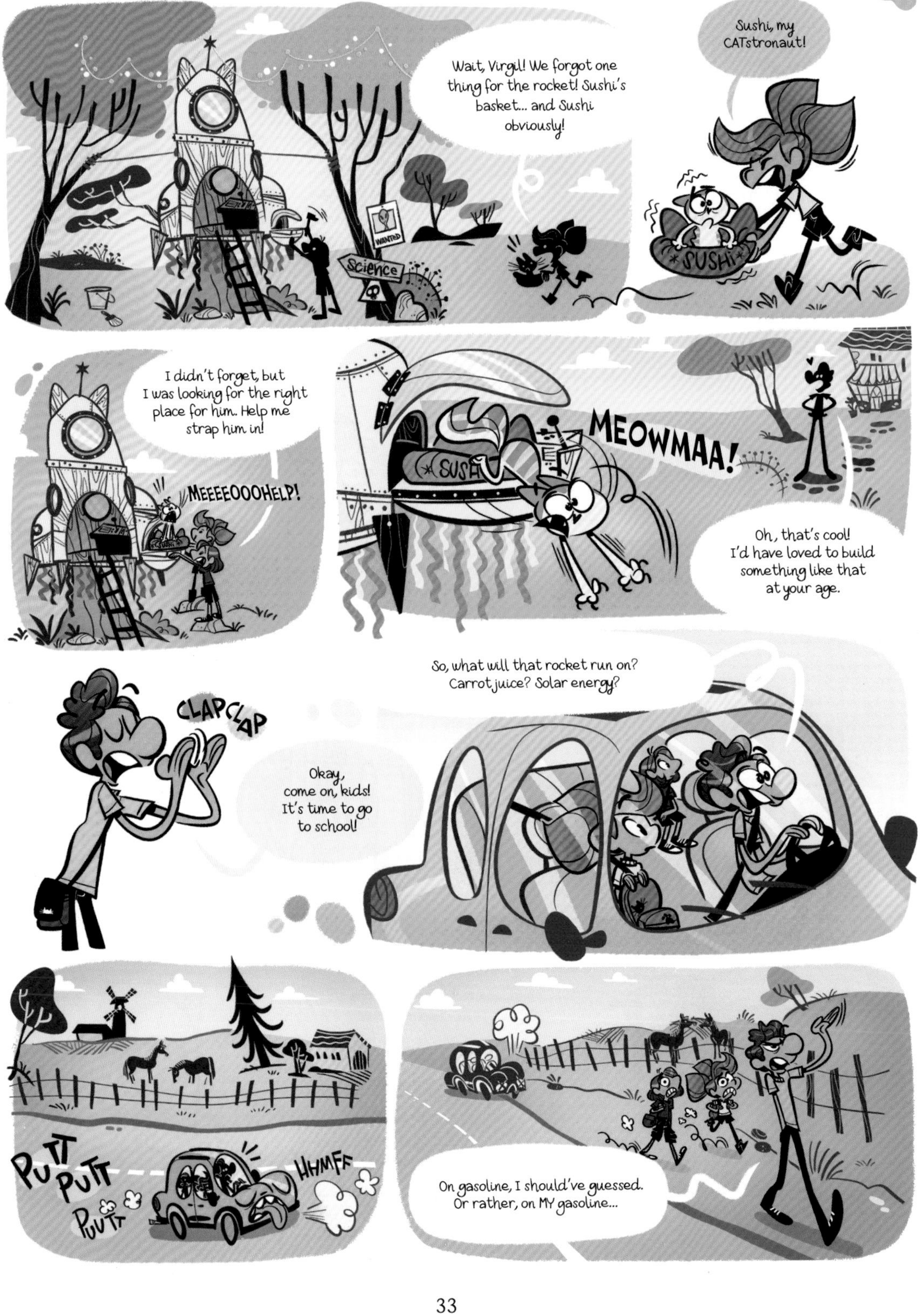
Wait, Virgil! We forgot one thing for the rocket! Sushi's basket... and Sushi obviously!
Sushi, my CATstronaut!
SUSHI
WANTED
Science
I didn't forget, but I was looking for the right place for him. Help me strap him in!
MEEEEOOOHELP!
MEOWMAA!
Oh, that's cool! I'd have loved to build something like that at your age.
So, what will that rocket run on? Carrot juice? Solar energy?
CLAPCLAP
Okay, come on, kids! It's time to go to school!
PUTT PUTT PUTT
HHMFF
On gasoline, I should've guessed. Or rather, on MY gasoline...

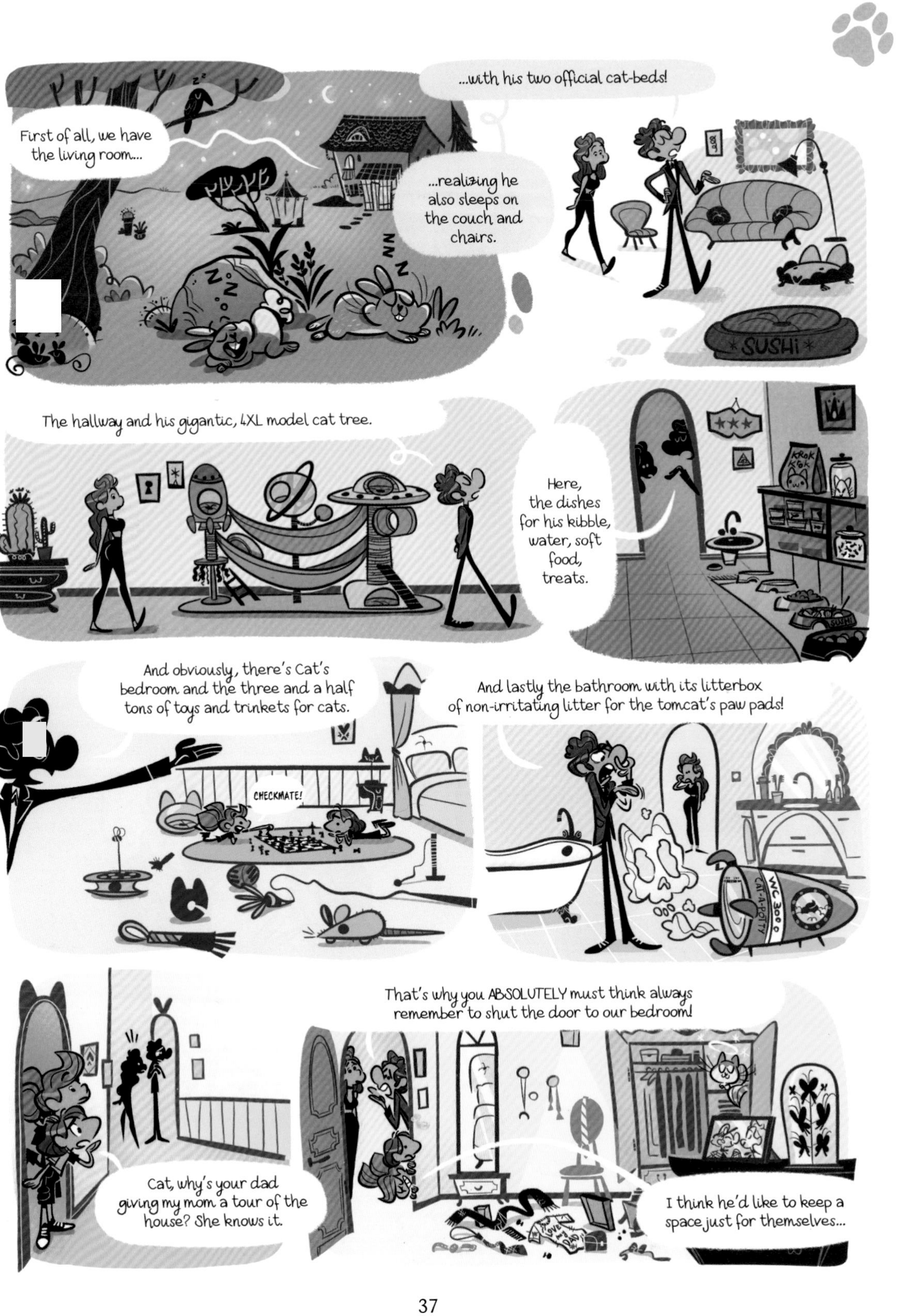
First of all, we have the living room...
...with his two official cat-beds!
...realizing he also sleeps on the couch and chairs.
SUSHI
The hallway and his gigantic, 4XL model cat tree.
Here, the dishes for his kibble, water, soft food, treats.
KROK KROK
And obviously, there's Cat's bedroom and the three and a half tons of toys and trinkets for cats.
CHECKMATE!
And lastly the bathroom with its litterbox of non-irritating litter for the tomcat's paw pads!
WC 3000
CAT-A-POTTY
That's why you ABSOLUTELY must think always remember to shut the door to our bedroom!
Cat, why's your dad giving my mom a tour of the house? She knows it.
I think he'd like to keep a space just for themselves...

Kids, we've called this family meeting to take stock of our life as a blended family.

INTERVENTION

At first, and it unsettled you, we fell in love during our camping trip.

"We saw each secretly. We realized we loved one another...

"Then we kicked it up a notch by taking you both on a trip to Venice...

"And we moved in together in Samantha's house. Today we want to go further..."
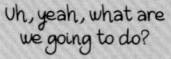

We want to prove we really are a family. Because a family means being united. In good or bad times.

Are you ready for that, kids?

Uh, yeah, what are we going to do?

An art gallery... can you believe it? They managed to drag us to an art gallery!

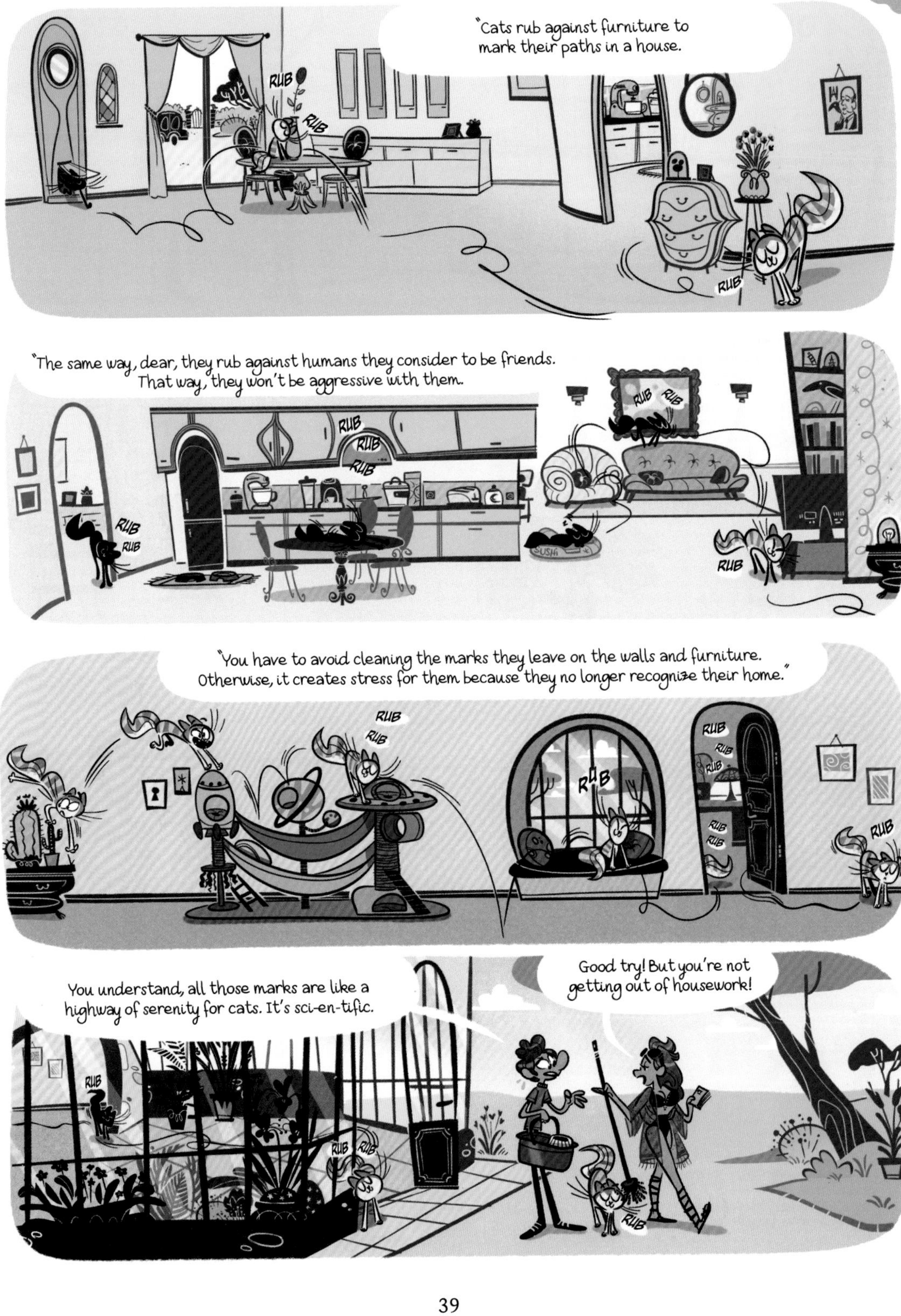
"Cats rub against furniture to mark their paths in a house.
RUB
RUB
RUB
"The same way, dear, they rub against humans they consider to be friends. That way, they won't be aggressive with them.
RUB RUB
RUB RUB RUB
RUB RUB
RUB
"You have to avoid cleaning the marks they leave on the walls and furniture. Otherwise, it creates stress for them because they no longer recognize their home."
RUB RUB
RUB
RUB RUB RUB
RUB RUB
RUB
You understand, all those marks are like a highway of serenity for cats. It's sci-en-tific.
Good try! But you're not getting out of housework!
RUB
RUB RUB
RUB

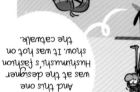

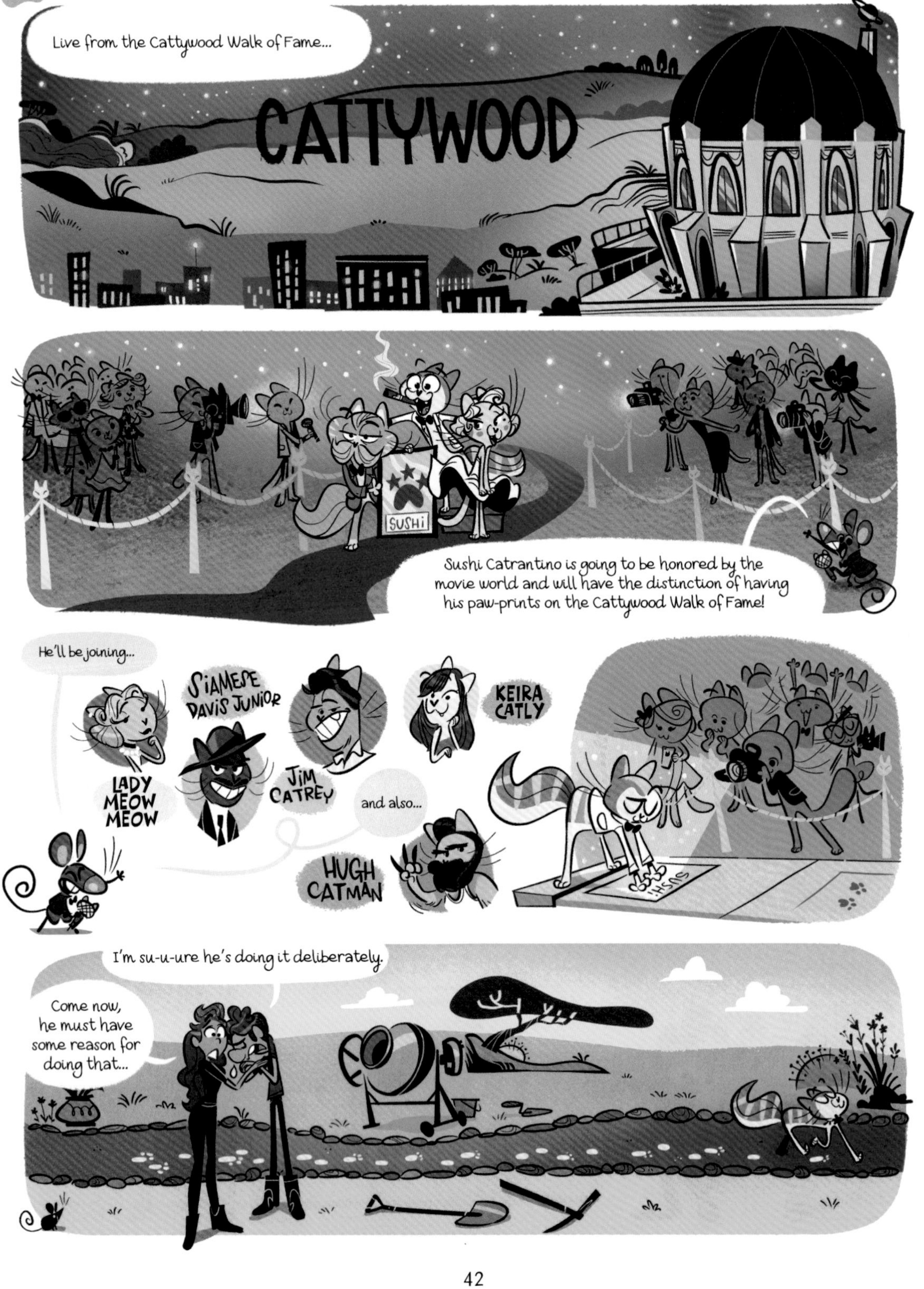
Live from the Cattywood Walk of Fame...
CATTYWOOD
SUSHi
Sushi Catrantino is going to be honored by the movie world and will have the distinction of having his paw-prints on the Cattywood Walk of Fame!
He'll be joining...
SIAMESE DAVIS JUNIOR
KEIRA CATLY
LADY MEOW MEOW
JIM CATREY
and also...
HUGH CATMAN
SUSHi
I'm su-u-ure he's doing it deliberately.
Come now, he must have some reason for doing that...

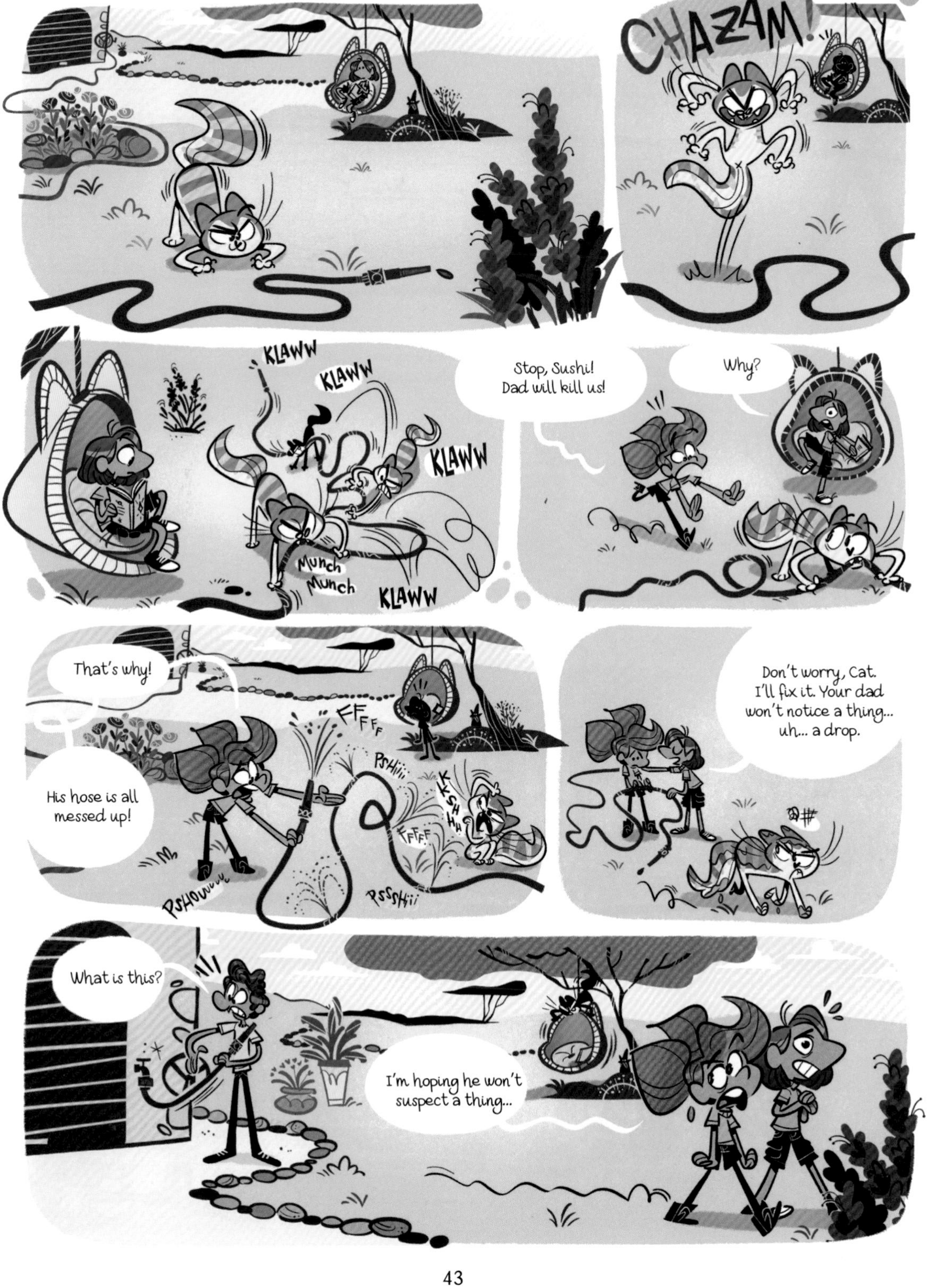
CHAZAM!
KLAWW
KLAWW
KLAWW
Munch
Munch
KLAWW
Stop, Sushi! Dad will kill us!
Why?
That's why!
His hose is all messed up!
FFFFF
PSHiii
KKSHHA
FFFFF
PSHOWWW
PSSSHiii
Don't worry, Cat. I'll fix it. Your dad won't notice a thing... uh... a drop.
What is this?
I'm hoping he won't suspect a thing...

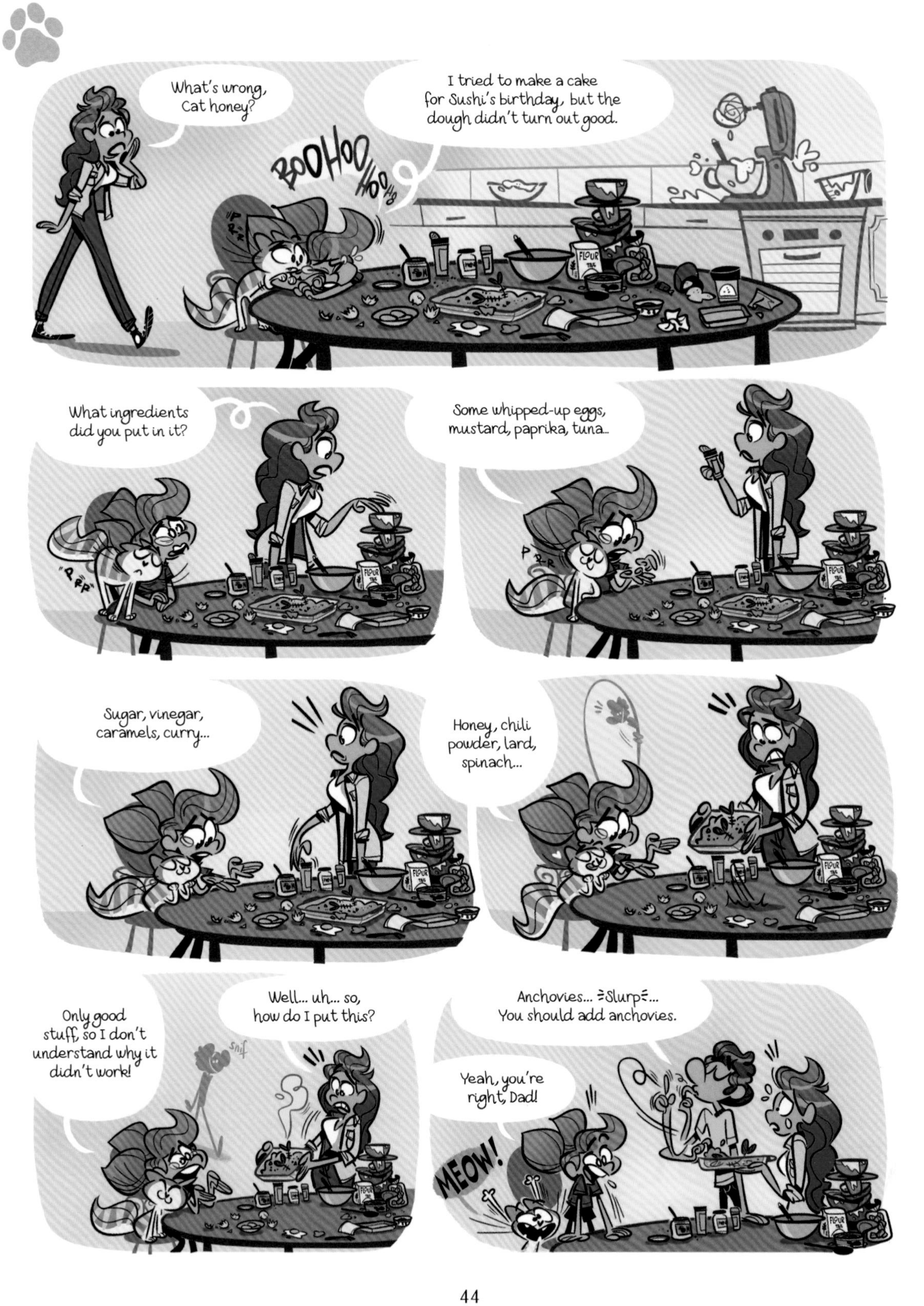
What's wrong, Cat honey?
I tried to make a cake for Sushi's birthday, but the dough didn't turn out good.
BOOHOO HOO
What ingredients did you put in it?
Some whipped-up eggs, mustard, paprika, tuna...
Sugar, vinegar, caramels, curry...
Honey, chili powder, lard, spinach...
Only good stuff, so I don't understand why it didn't work!
Well... uh... so, how do I put this?
snif
Anchovies... ≡Slurp≡... You should add anchovies.
Yeah, you're right, Dad!
MEOW!

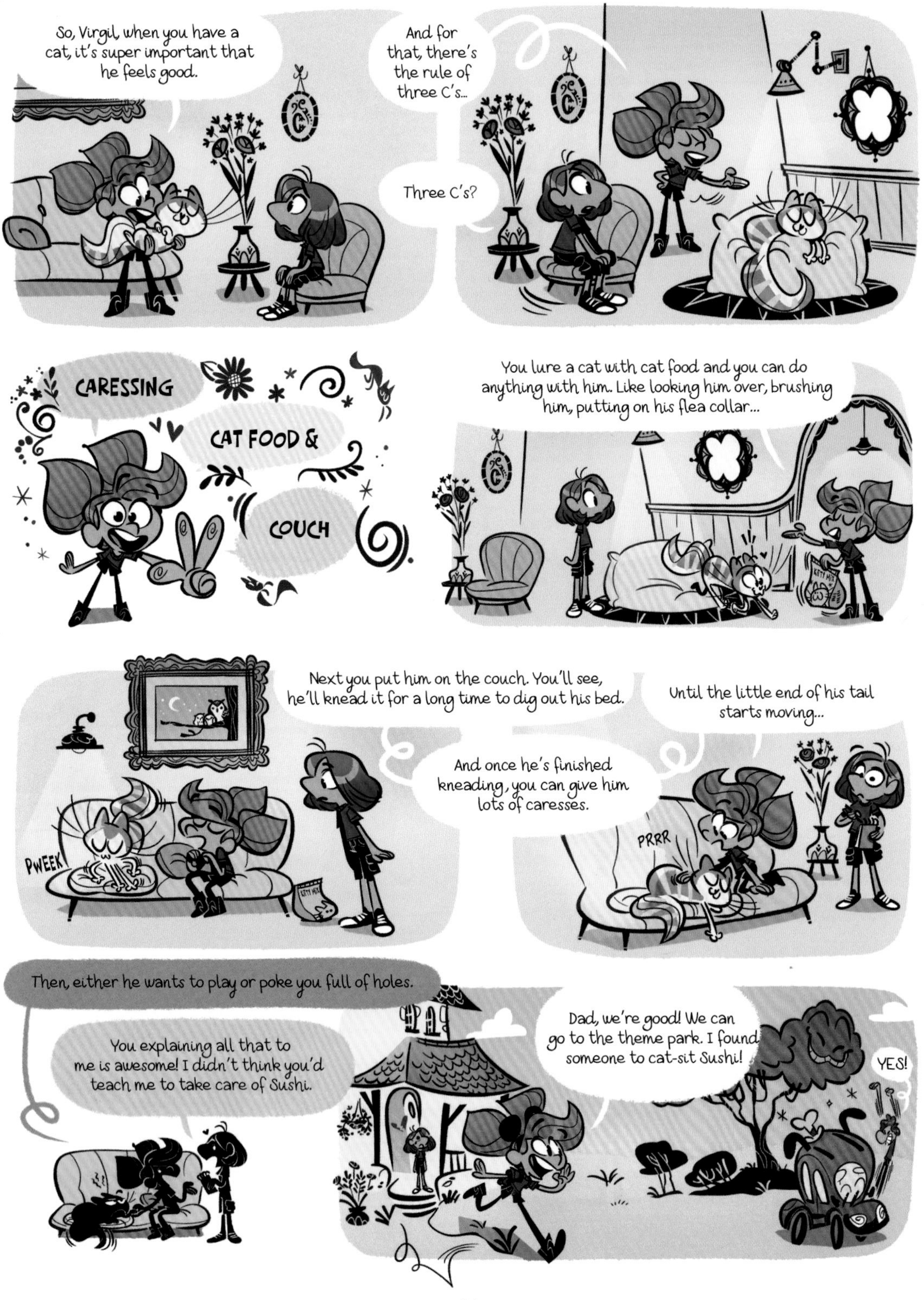

So, Virgil, when you have a cat, it's super important that he feels good.
And for that, there's the rule of three C's...
Three C's?
CARESSING
CAT FOOD &
COUCH
You lure a cat with cat food and you can do anything with him. Like looking him over, brushing him, putting on his flea collar...
Next you put him on the couch. You'll see, he'll knead it for a long time to dig out his bed.
PWEEK
And once he's finished kneading, you can give him lots of caresses.
Until the little end of his tail starts moving...
PRRR
Then, either he wants to play or poke you full of holes.
You explaining all that to me is awesome! I didn't think you'd teach me to take care of Sushi.
Dad, we're good! We can go to the theme park. I found someone to cat-sit Sushi!
YES!

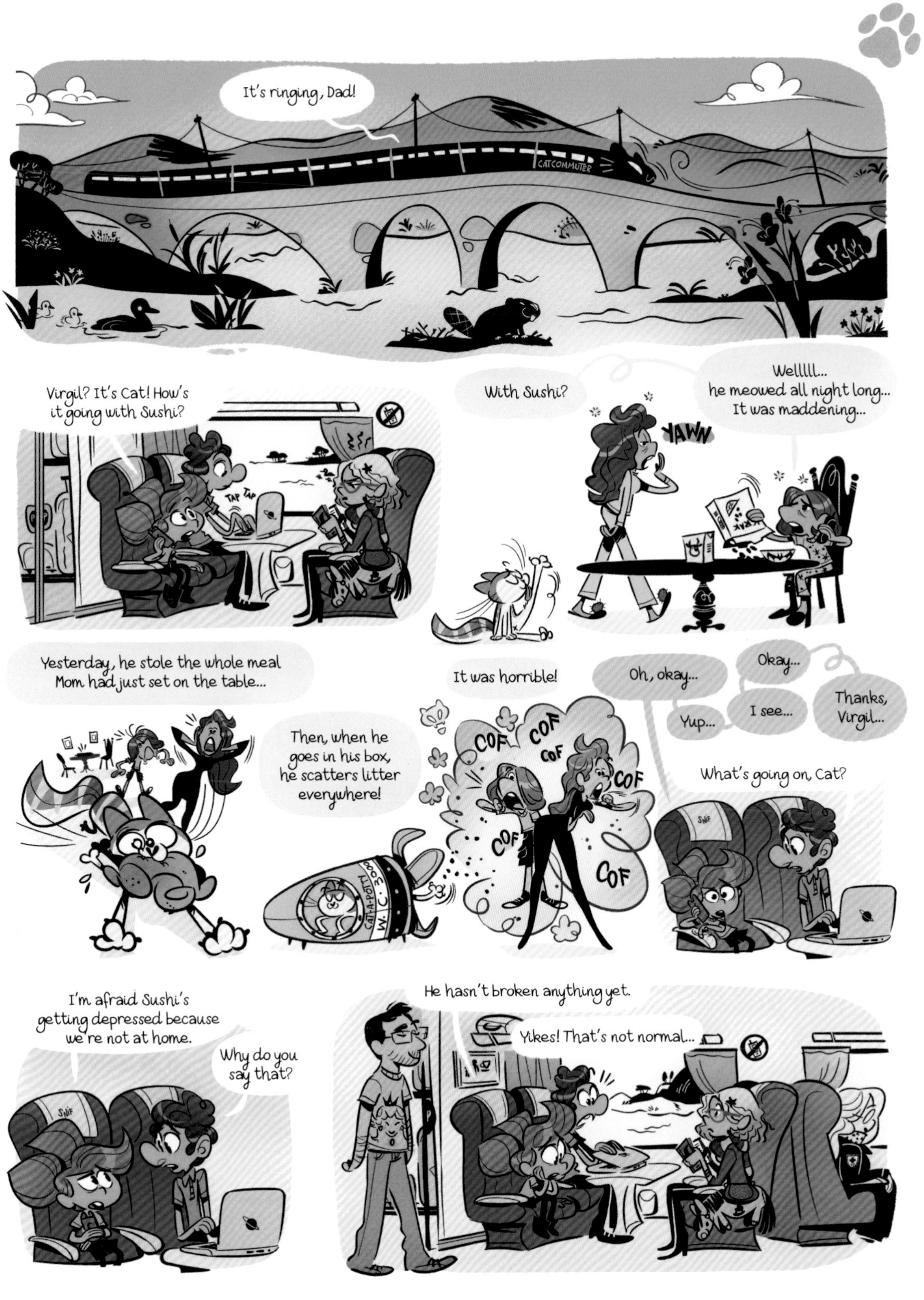
It's ringing, Dad!
CATCOMMUTER
Virgil? It's Cat! How's it going with Sushi?
TAP TAP
With Sushi?
Wellllll... he meowed all night long... It was maddening...
YAWN
Yesterday, he stole the whole meal Mom had just set on the table...
Then, when he goes in his box, he scatters litter everywhere!
CAT-A-POTTY W.C. 3000
It was horrible!
COF COF COF COF COF COF
Oh, okay...
Okay...
Yup...
I see...
Thanks, Virgil...
What's going on, Cat?
I'm afraid Sushi's getting depressed because we're not at home.
Why do you say that?
He hasn't broken anything yet.
Yikes! That's not normal...

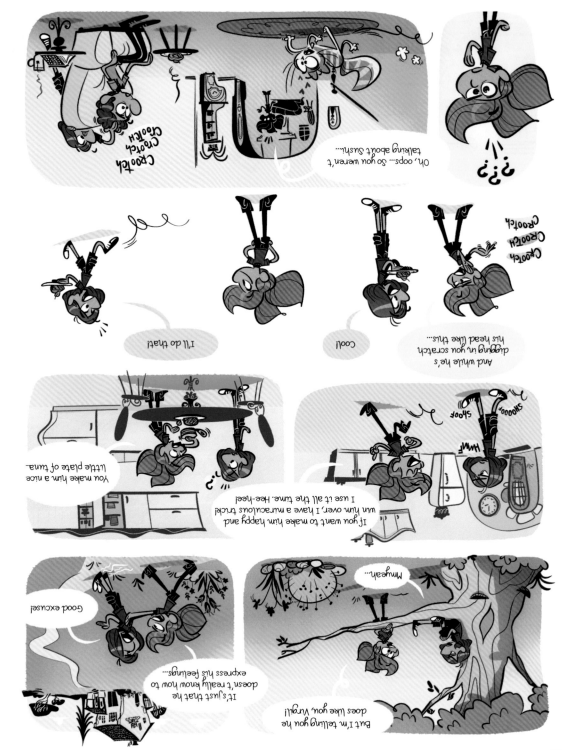

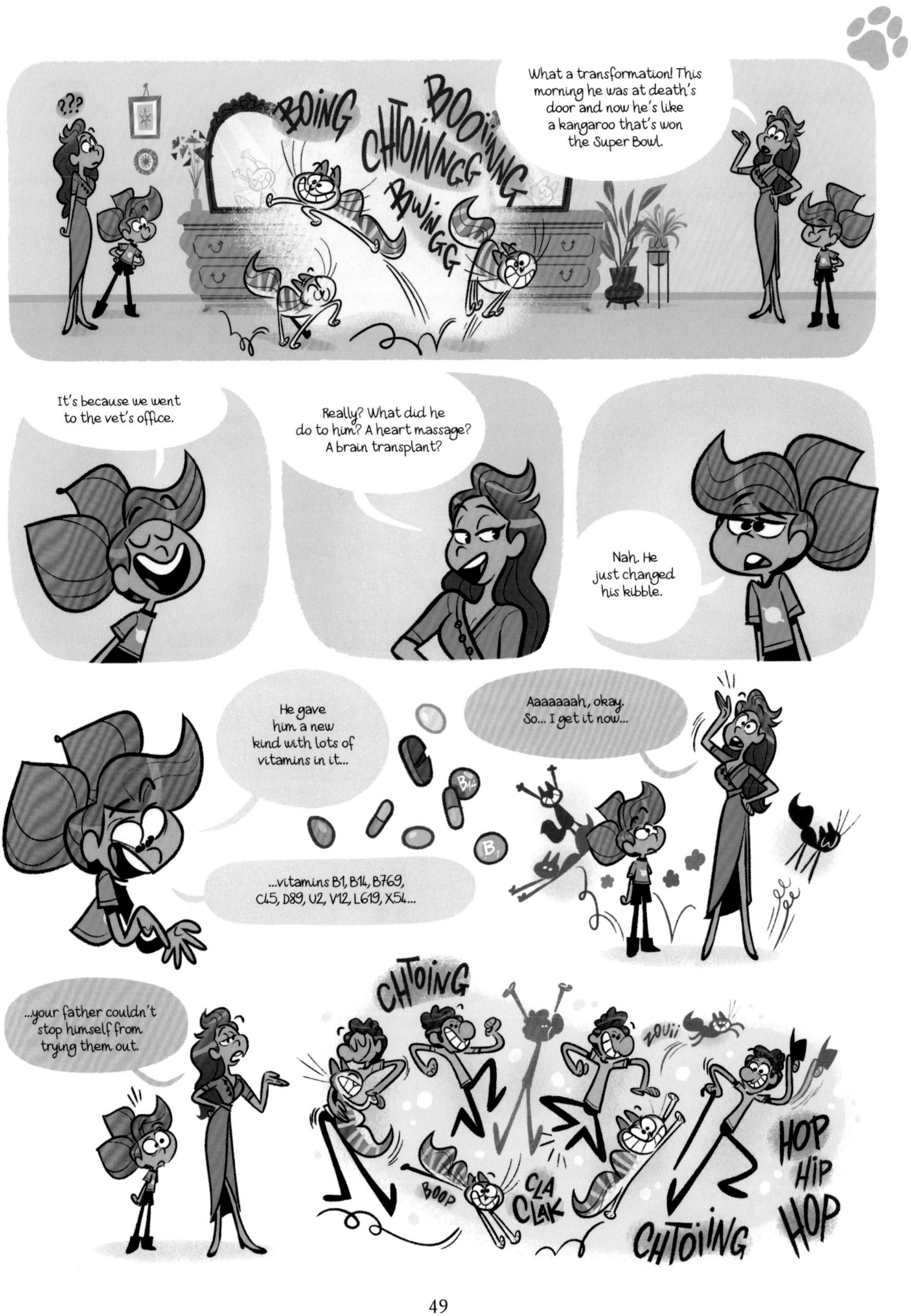

???
BOING
BOOÏNNG
CHTOINNGG
BWINGG
What a transformation! This morning he was at death's door and now he's like a kangaroo that's won the Super Bowl.
It's because we went to the vet's office.
Really? What did he do to him? A heart massage? A brain transplant?
Nah. He just changed his kibble.
He gave him a new kind with lots of vitamins in it...
...vitamins B1, B14, B769, C45, D89, U2, V12, L619, X54...
Aaaaaah, okay. So... I get it now...
...your father couldn't stop himself from trying them out.
CHTOING
ZOUII
BOOP
CLA CLAK
CHTOIING
HOP HIP HOP

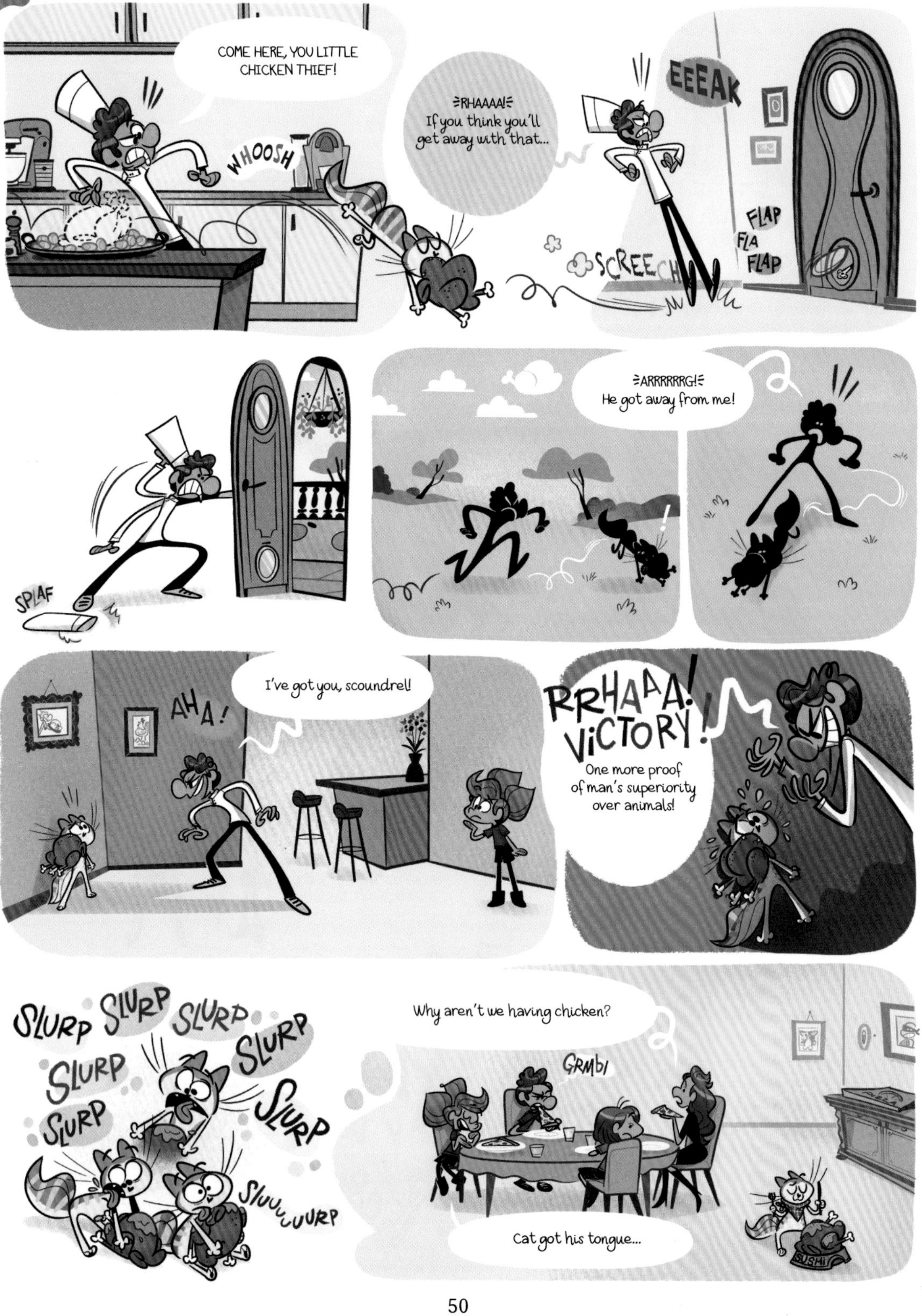
COME HERE, YOU LITTLE CHICKEN THIEF!
WHOOSH
≡RHAAAA!≡ If you think you'll get away with that...
EEEAK
SCREECH
FLAP
FLA
FLAP
SPLAF
≡ARRRRRRG!≡ He got away from me!
I've got you, scoundrel!
AHA!
RRHAAA! VICTORY!
One more proof of man's superiority over animals!
SLURP
SLURP
SLURP
SLURP
SLURP
SLURP
SLURP
SLUUUUURP
Why aren't we having chicken?
GRMBl
Cat got his tongue...
SUSHI

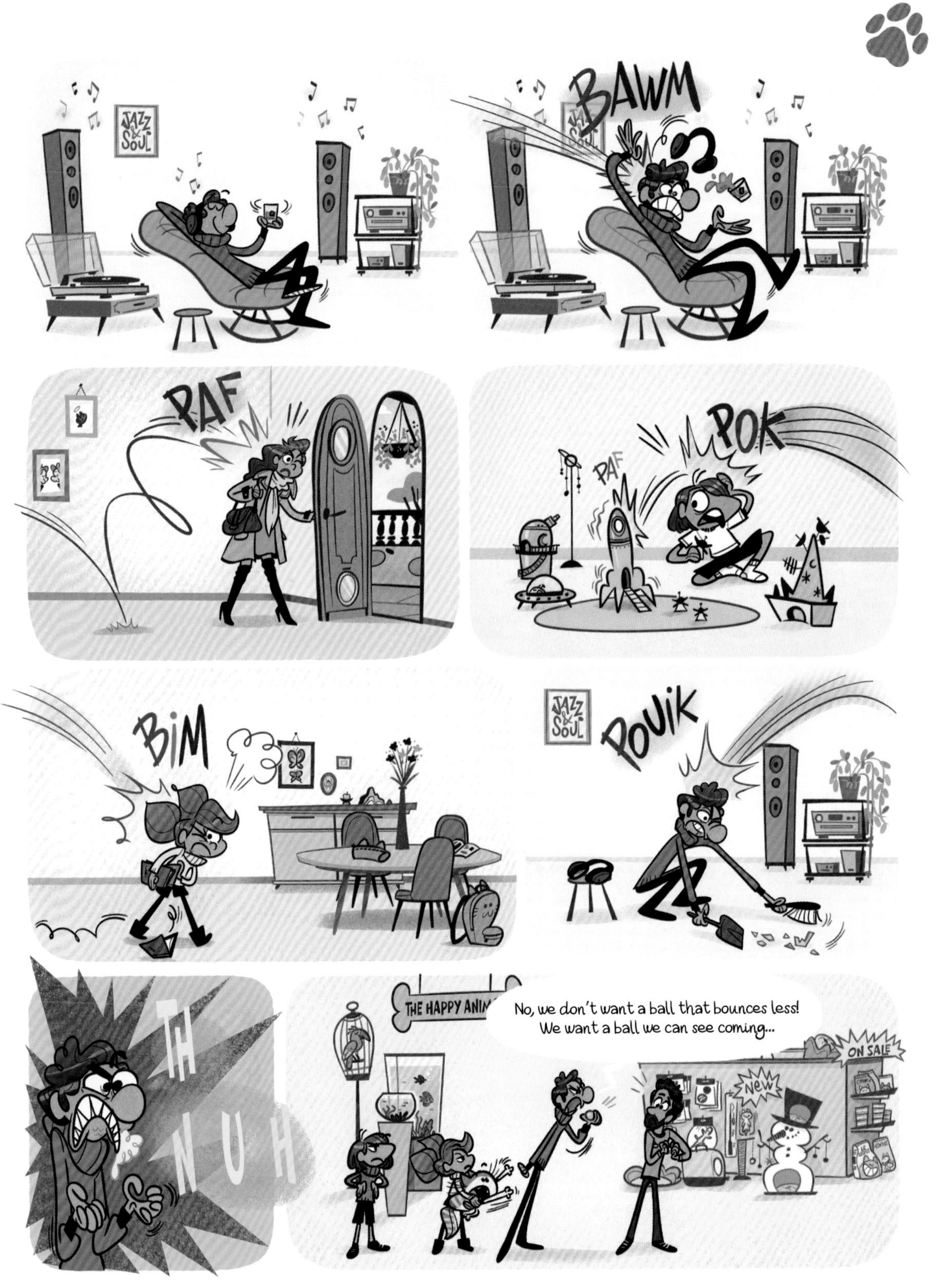
JAZZ & SOUL
BAWM
JAZZ & SOUL
PAF
PAF
POK
BIM
JAZZ & SOUL
POUIK
TH
NUH
THE HAPPY ANIM
No, we don't want a ball that bounces less!
We want a ball we can see coming...
NEW
ON SALE

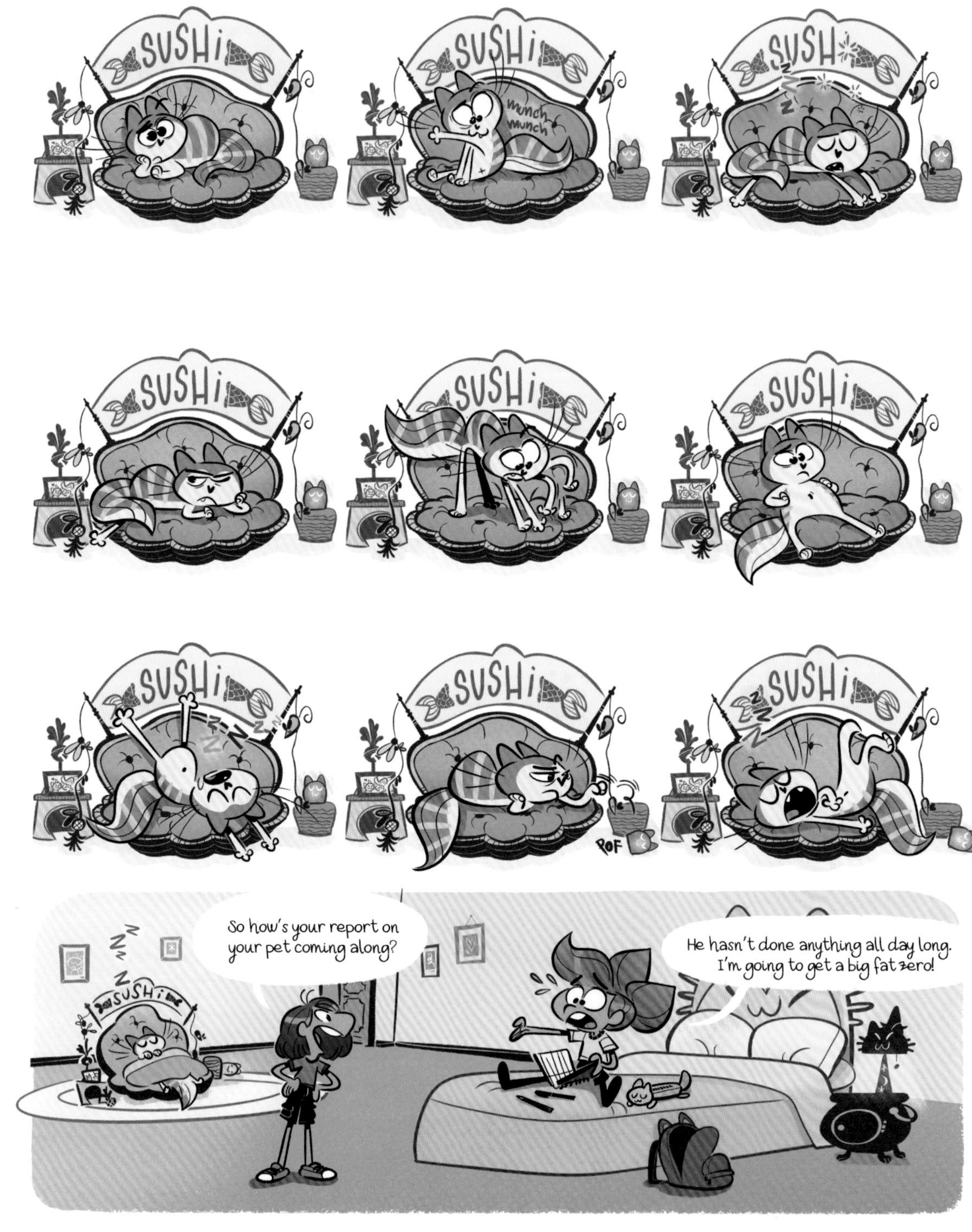
SUSHI
munch munch
POF
So how's your report on your pet coming along?
He hasn't done anything all day long. I'm going to get a big fat zero!

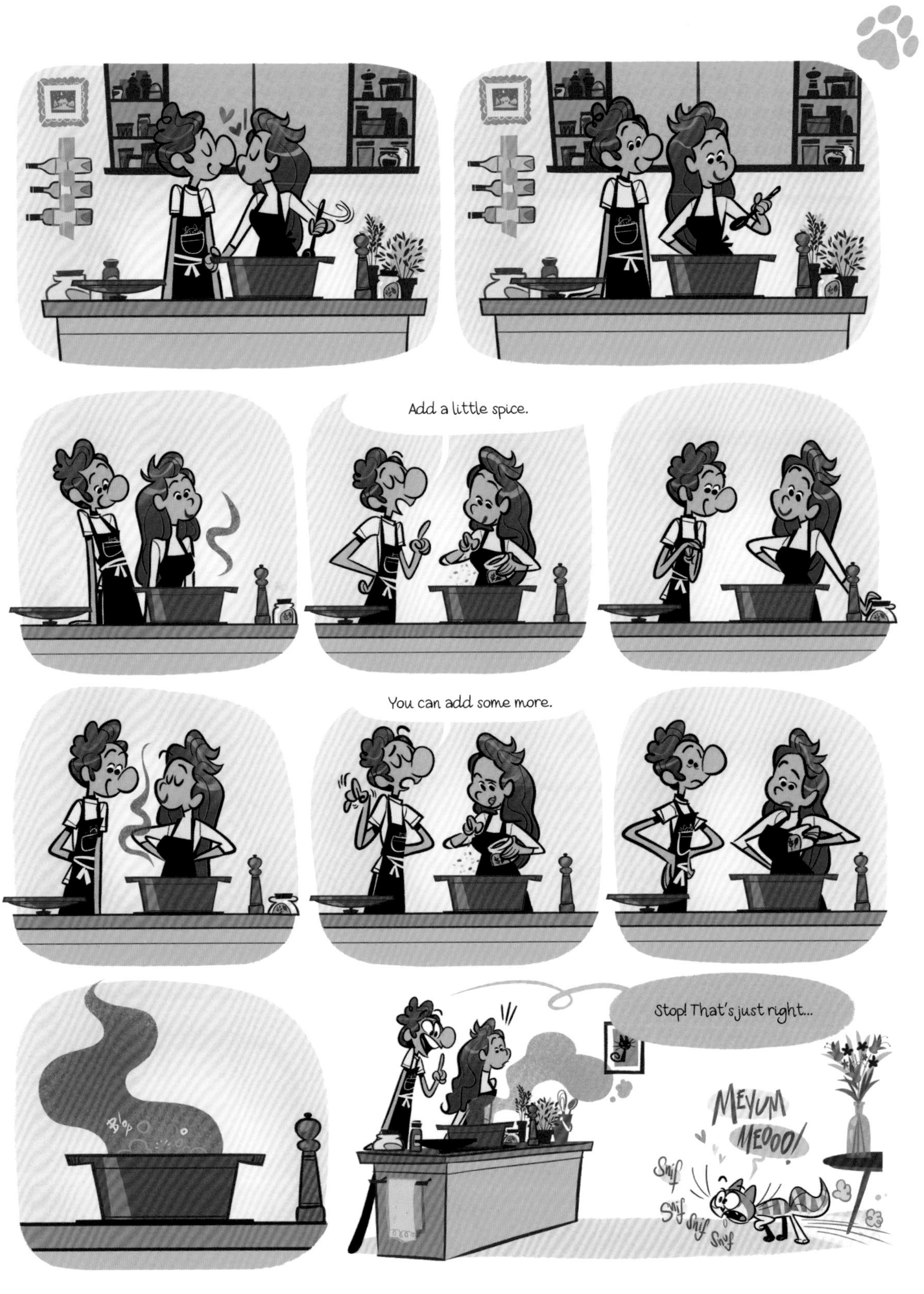
Add a little spice.
You can add some more.
Blop
Stop! That's just right...
MEYUM
MEOOO!
Snif
Snif
Snif
Snif
Snif

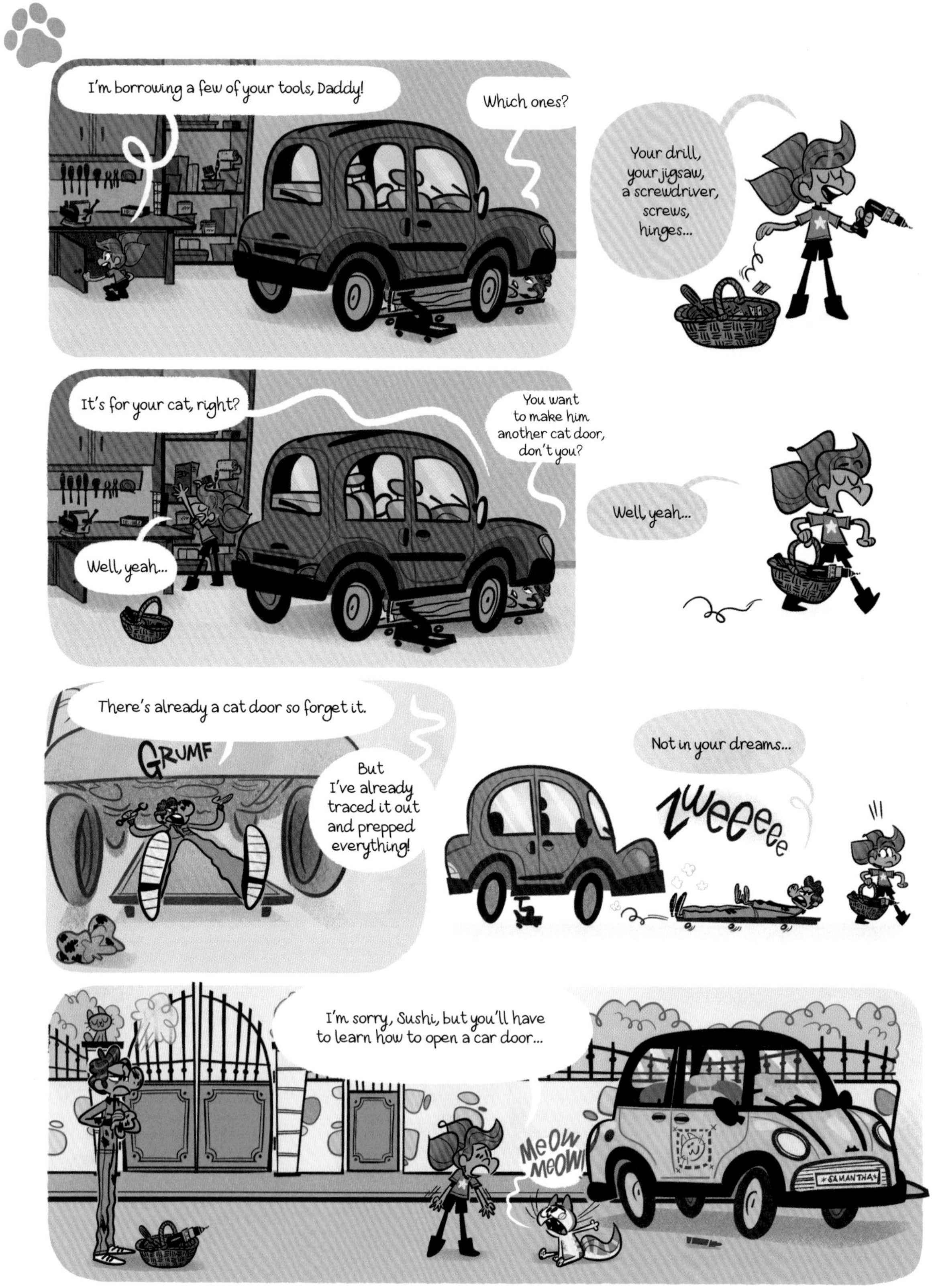
I'm borrowing a few of your tools, Daddy!
Which ones?
Your drill, your jigsaw, a screwdriver, screws, hinges...
It's for your cat, right?
You want to make him another cat door, don't you?
Well, yeah...
Well, yeah...
There's already a cat door so forget it.
GRUMF
But I've already traced it out and prepped everything!
Not in your dreams...
ZWEEEEE
I'm sorry, Sushi, but you'll have to learn how to open a car door...
MEOW MEOW!
SAMANTHA

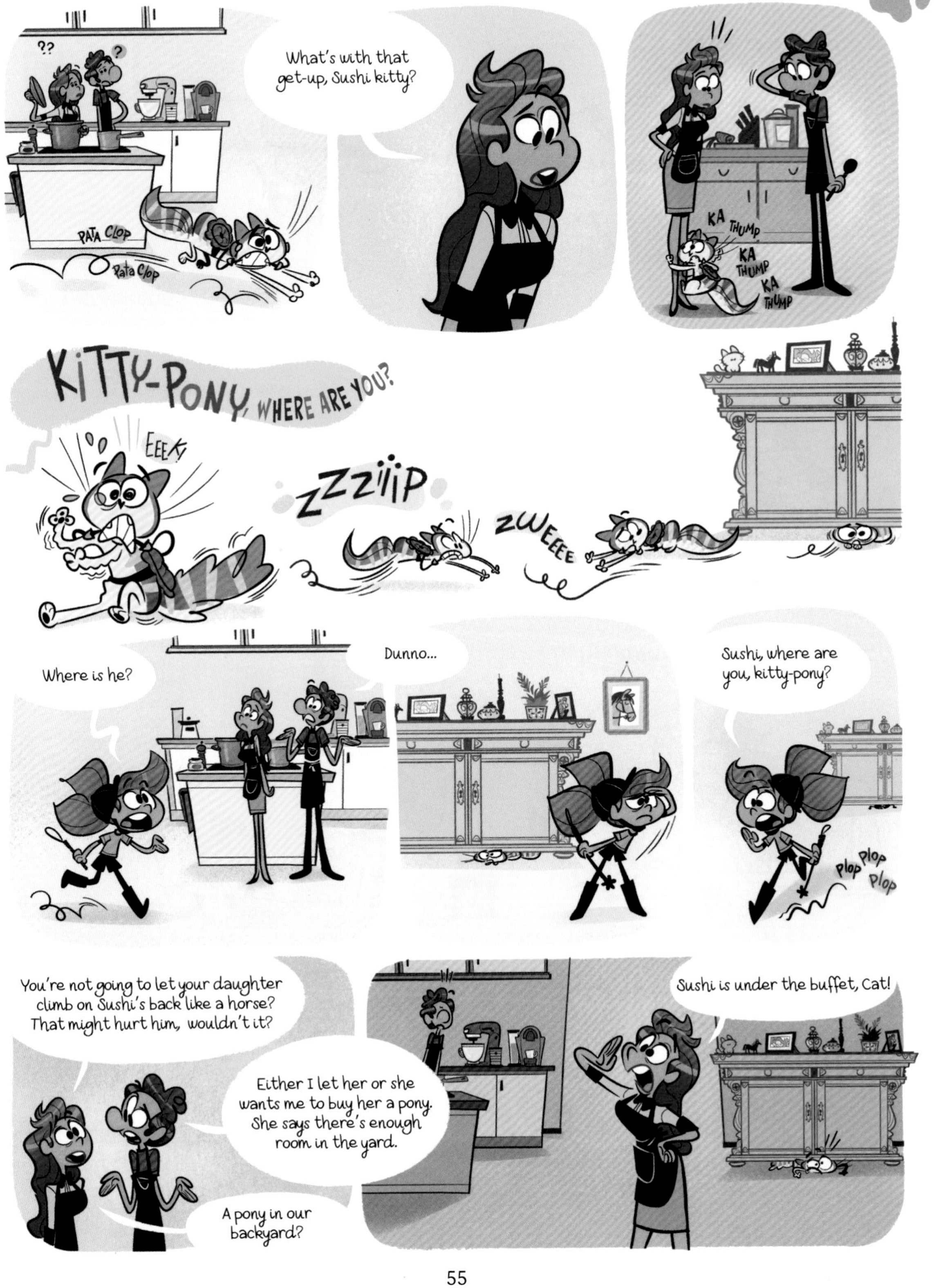
??
?
What's with that get-up, Sushi kitty?
PATA CLOP
Pata Clop
KA THUMP
KA THUMP
KA THUMP
KITTY-PONY, WHERE ARE YOU?
EEEK!
ZZZIIIP
ZWEEEE
Where is he?
Dunno...
Sushi, where are you, kitty-pony?
Plop Plop Plop
You're not going to let your daughter climb on Sushi's back like a horse? That might hurt him, wouldn't it?
Either I let her or she wants me to buy her a pony. She says there's enough room in the yard.
A pony in our backyard?
Sushi is under the buffet, Cat!

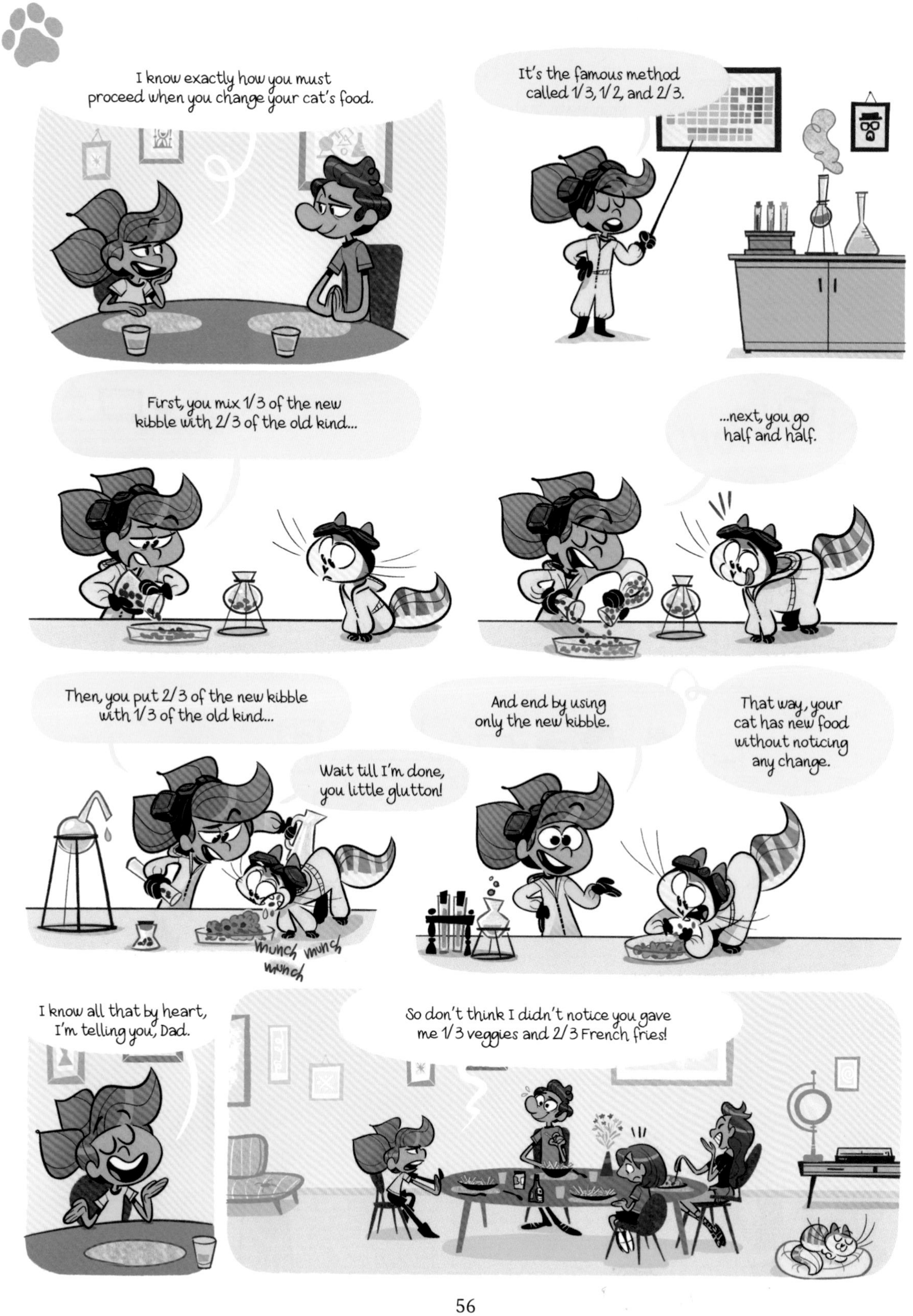
I know exactly how you must proceed when you change your cat's food.
It's the famous method called 1/3, 1/2, and 2/3.
First, you mix 1/3 of the new kibble with 2/3 of the old kind...
...next, you go half and half.
Then, you put 2/3 of the new kibble with 1/3 of the old kind...
Wait till I'm done, you little glutton!
munch munch munch
And end by using only the new kibble.
That way, your cat has new food without noticing any change.
I know all that by heart, I'm telling you, Dad.
So don't think I didn't notice you gave me 1/3 veggies and 2/3 French fries!

Cat, hurry up! We're going! Everyone is waiting on you!
I can't, Daddy! Sushi won't come out!
What's the problem?! He's not coming with us anyhow.
The problem is his sixth sense! Nothing can get him to come out.
At a minimum, we'll be in a car accident or get robbed! We got to listen to Sushi. We can't leave the house!
Cats sense catastrophes shortly before they happen. And this smells like a super catastrophe.
I think you're right.
STAYING HOME!
YES!
SUSHI! KIBBLE TIME!
ZZZOOOOOMM
Look, Cat, honey. That painting is titled "Sixth Sense Upside Down."
I sense I'm going to cause a catastrophe!

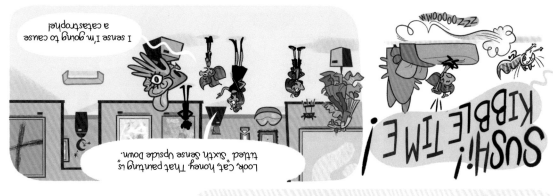

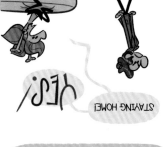

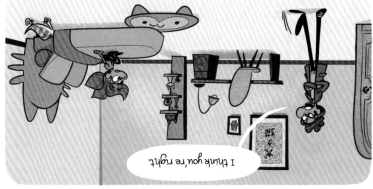

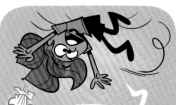

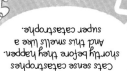

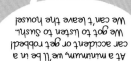

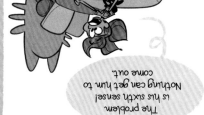

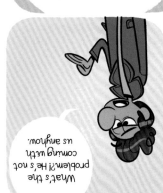

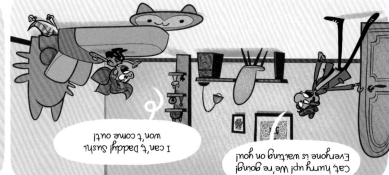

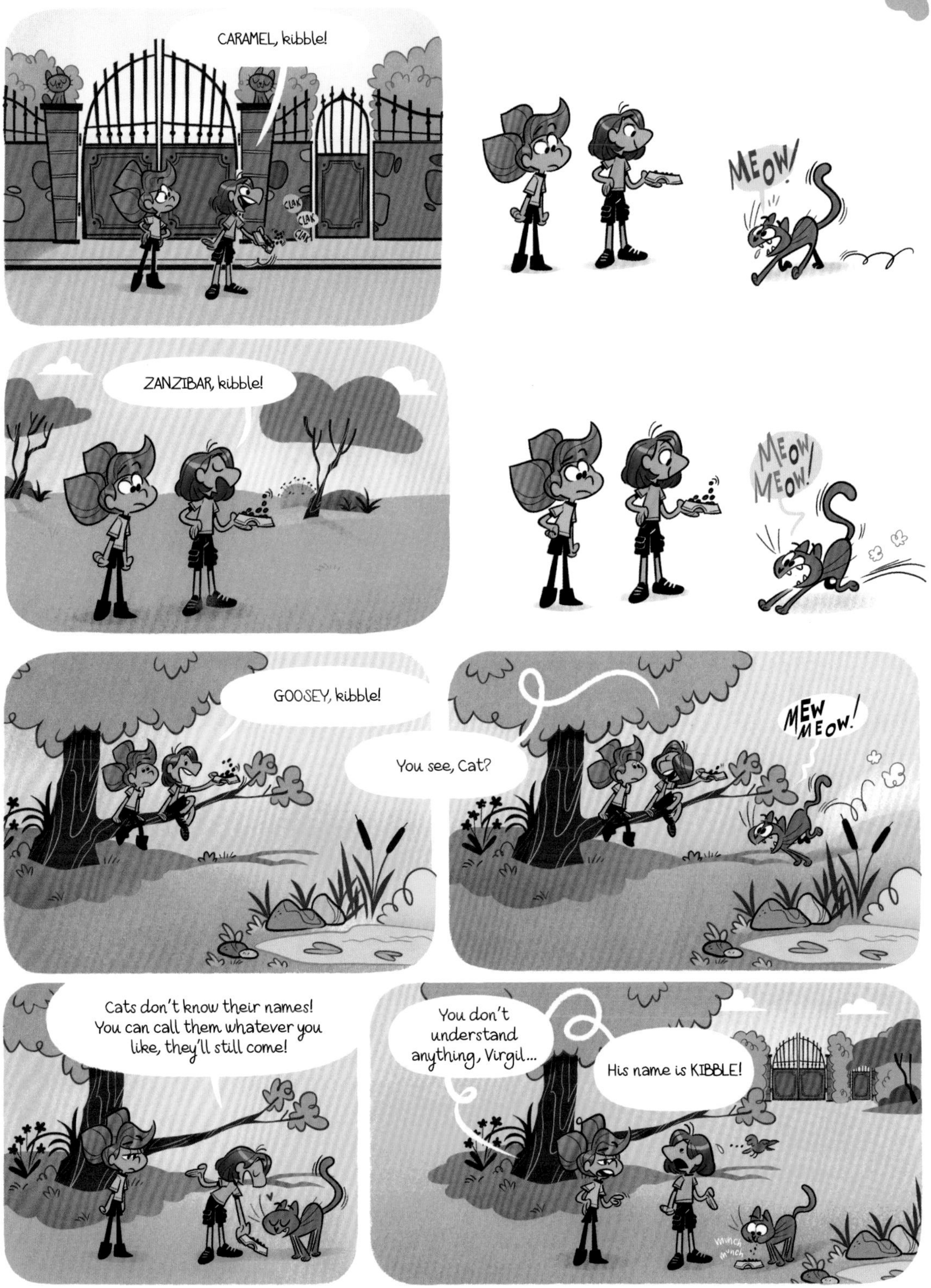
CARAMEL, kibble!
CLAK CLAK CLAK
MEOW!
ZANZIBAR, kibble!
MEOW MEOW!
GOOSEY, kibble!
You see, Cat?
MEW MEOW!
Cats don't know their names! You can call them whatever you like, they'll still come!
You don't understand anything, Virgil...
His name is KIBBLE!
munch munch

Will we stay in the same hotel as last time, Dad?

...but if we stay home, he'll drive us crazy with his loud meowing!

Hurry, hurry, he just figured it out!

Sushi isn't coming...

MiiAAA iiiOUUU!

You know a restaurant that'll serve cats?

Get dressed. We're going to a restaurant!

And all the stores are closed until tomorrow!

...there's not a single kibble left in the whole house!

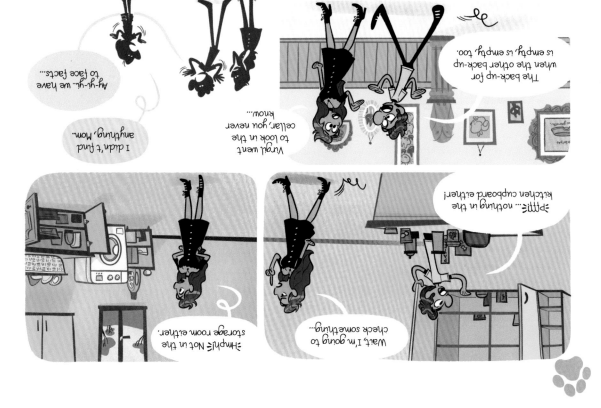

Ay-y-y... we have to face facts...

I didn't find anything, Mom.

Virgil went to look in the cellar, you never know...

The back-up for when the other back-up is empty, too.

Wait, I'm going to check something...

Humph! Nothing in the kitchen cupboard either!

Humph! Not in the storage room either.

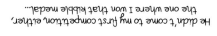

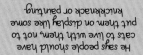

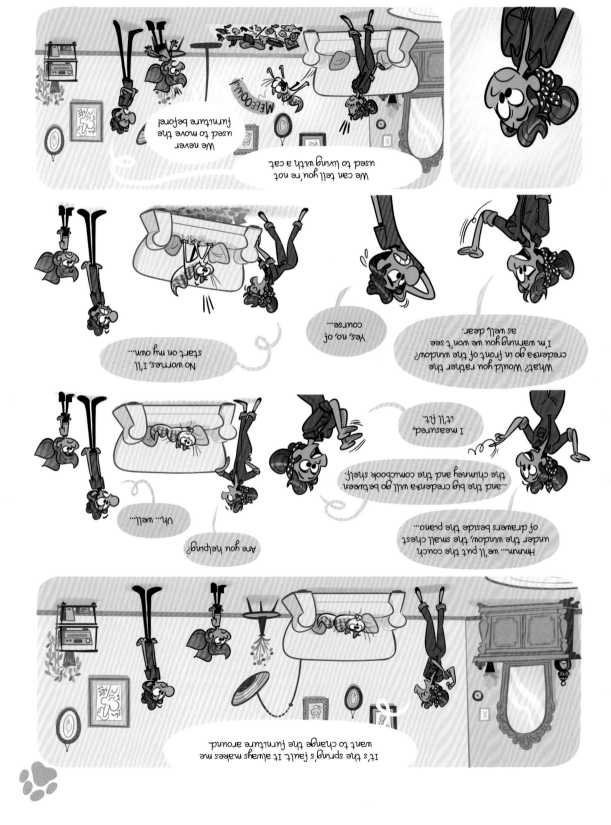

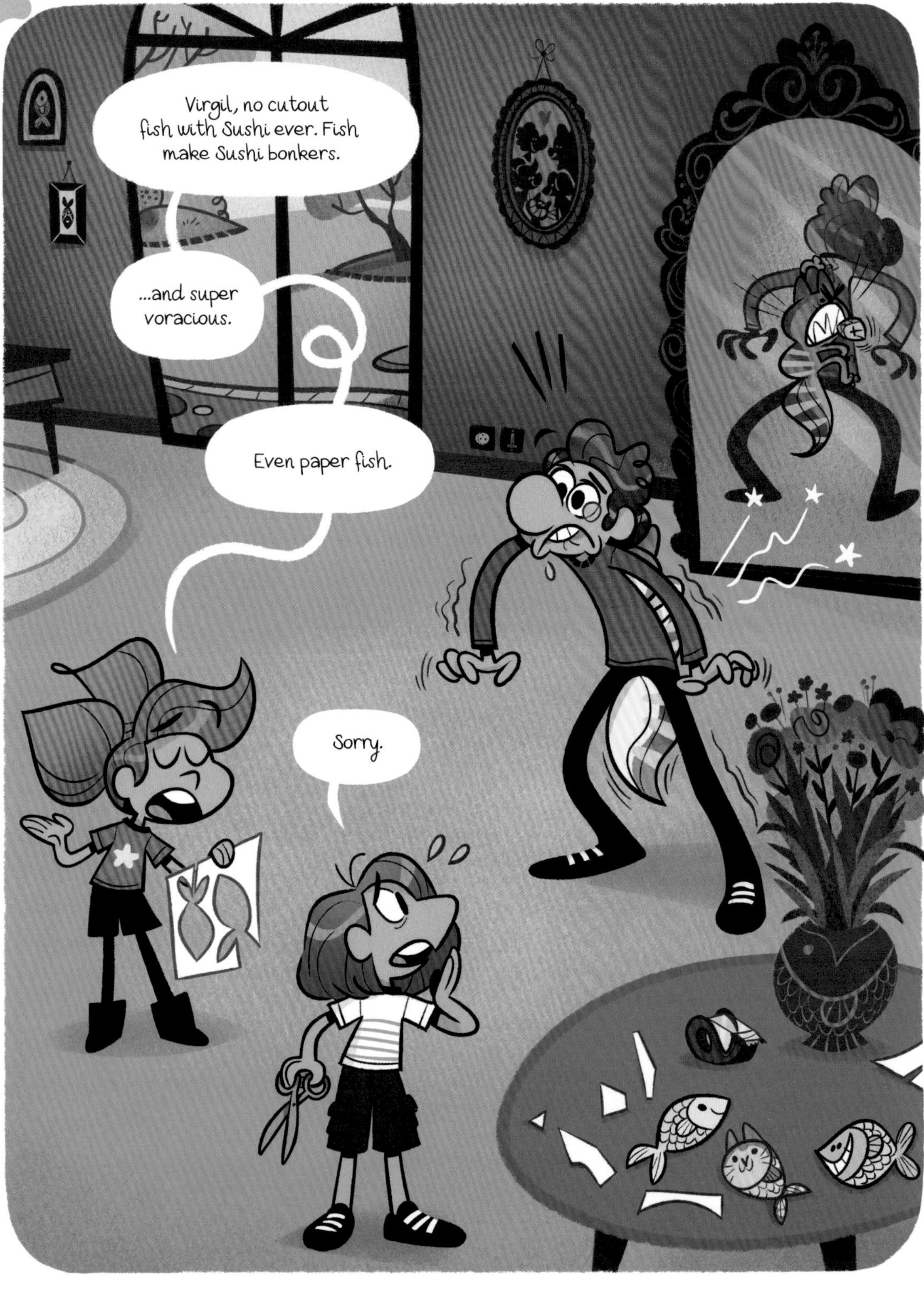
Virgil, no cutout fish with Sushi ever. Fish make Sushi bonkers.
...and super voracious.
Even paper fish.
Sorry.

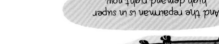

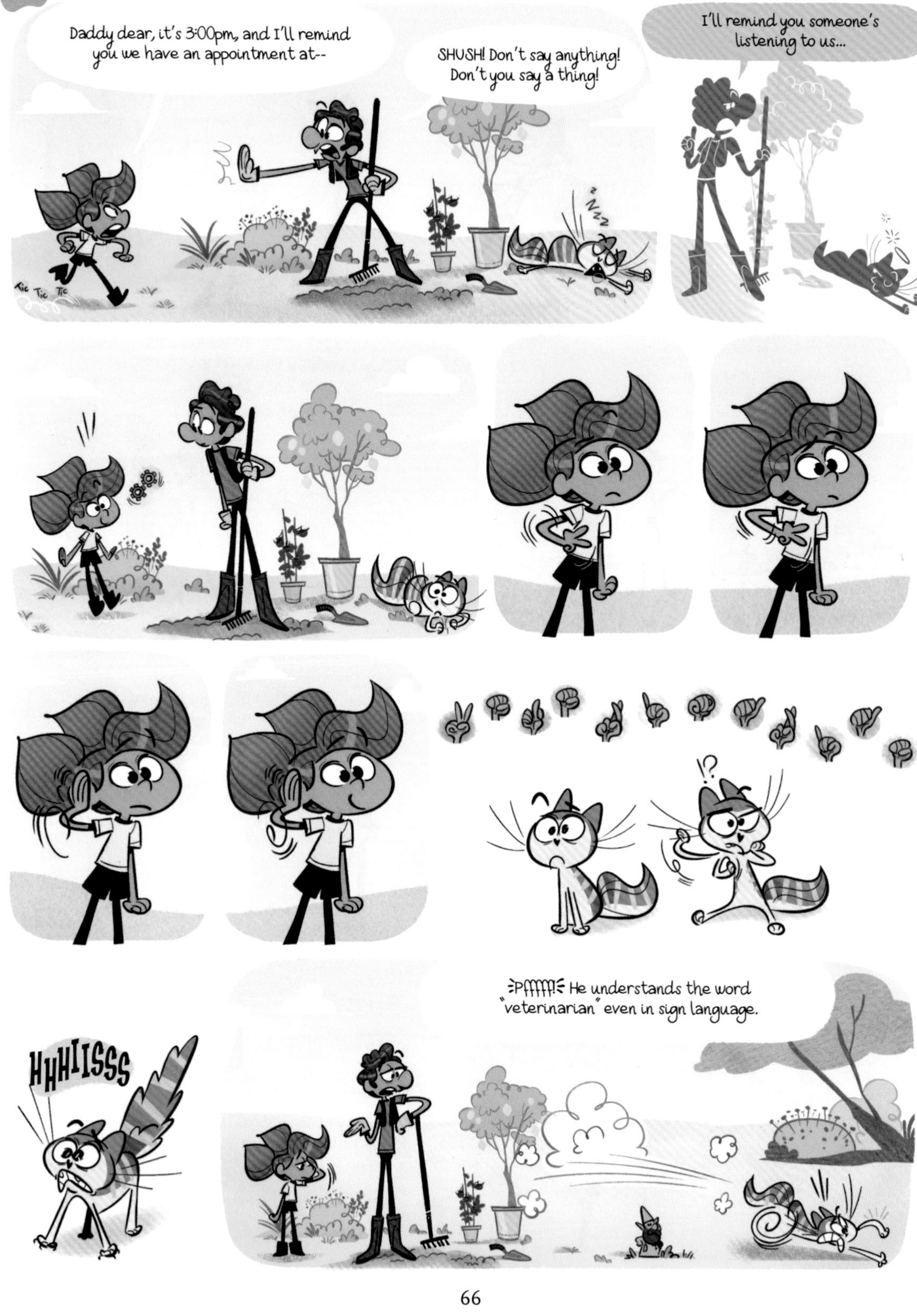
Daddy dear, it's 3:00pm, and I'll remind you we have an appointment at--
Tic Tic Tic
SHUSH! Don't say anything! Don't you say a thing!
I'll remind you someone's listening to us...
HHHIISSS
PFFFFF! He understands the word "veterinarian" even in sign language.

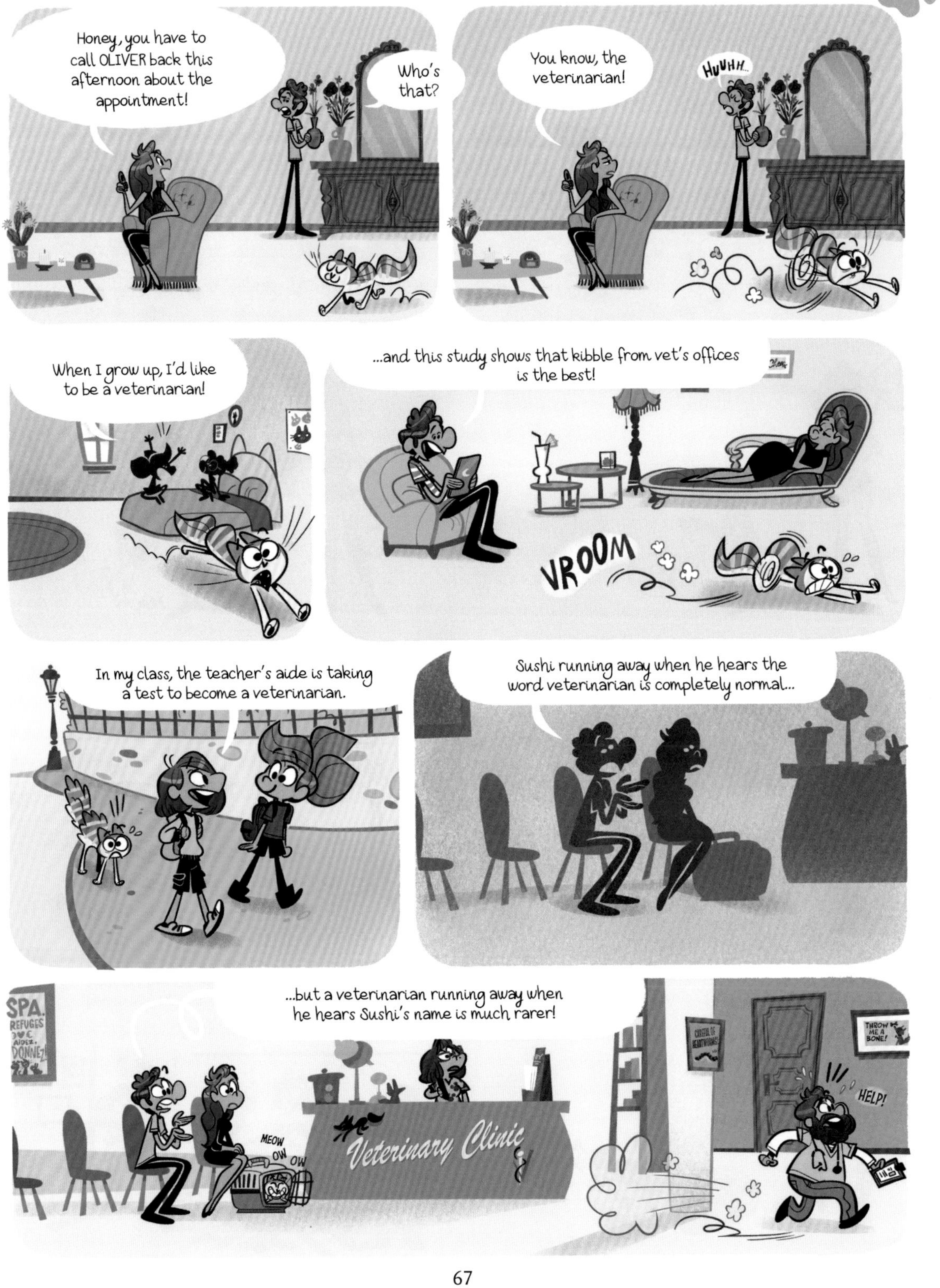
Honey, you have to call OLIVER back this afternoon about the appointment!
Who's that?
You know, the veterinarian!
HUUHH...
When I grow up, I'd like to be a veterinarian!
...and this study shows that kibble from vet's offices is the best!
VROOM
In my class, the teacher's aide is taking a test to become a veterinarian.
Sushi running away when he hears the word veterinarian is completely normal...
...but a veterinarian running away when he hears Sushi's name is much rarer!
SPA.
REFUGES
AIDEZ.
DONNEZ
MEOW
OW
OW
Veterinary Clinic
CAREFUL OF HEARTWORMS!
THROW ME A BONE!
HELP!

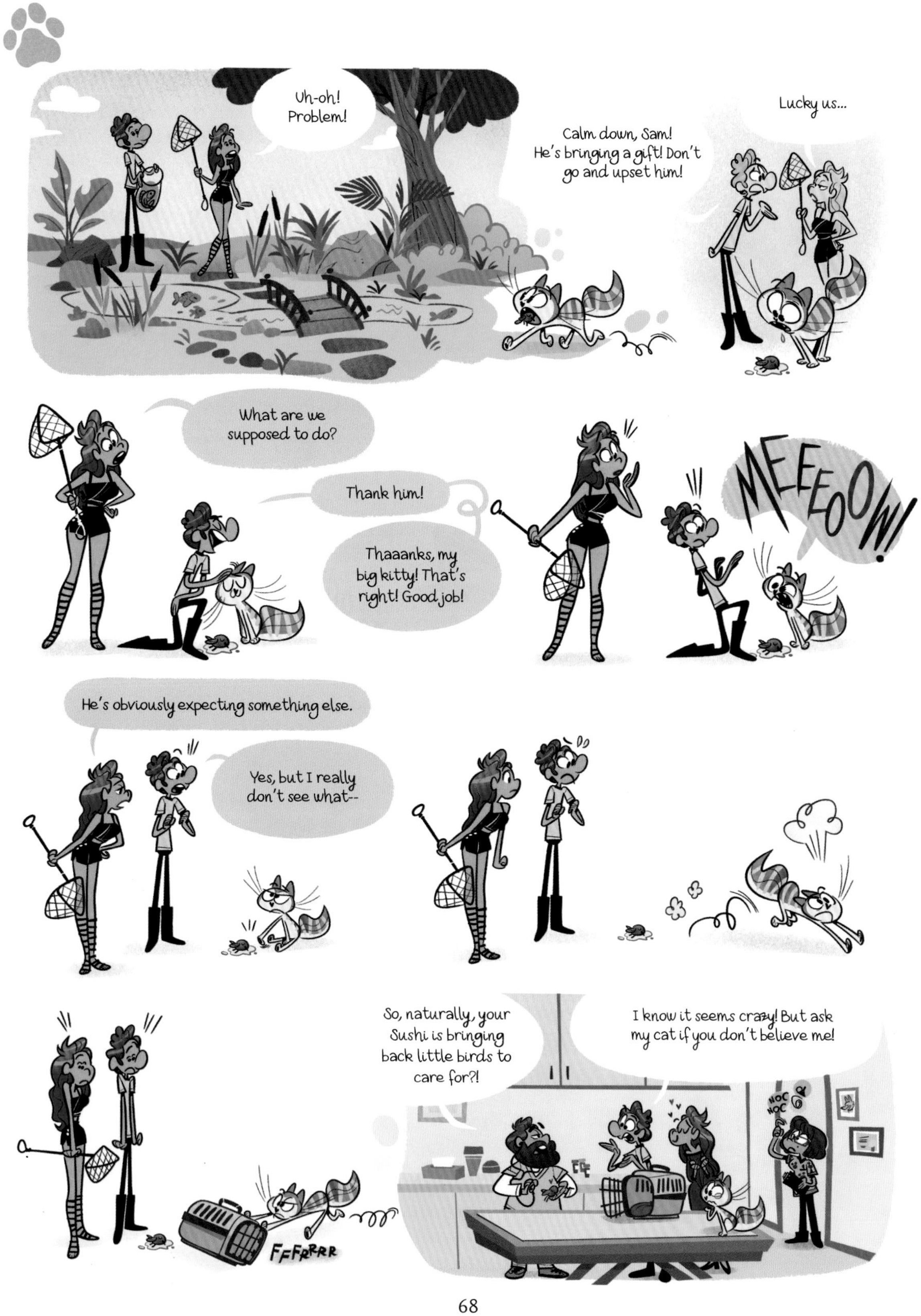
Uh-oh! Problem!
Calm down, Sam! He's bringing a gift! Don't go and upset him!
Lucky us...
What are we supposed to do?
Thank him!
Thaaanks, my big kitty! That's right! Good job!
MEEEOOW!
He's obviously expecting something else.
Yes, but I really don't see what--
FFFRRRR
So, naturally, your Sushi is bringing back little birds to care for?!
I know it seems crazy! But ask my cat if you don't believe me!
NOC NOC

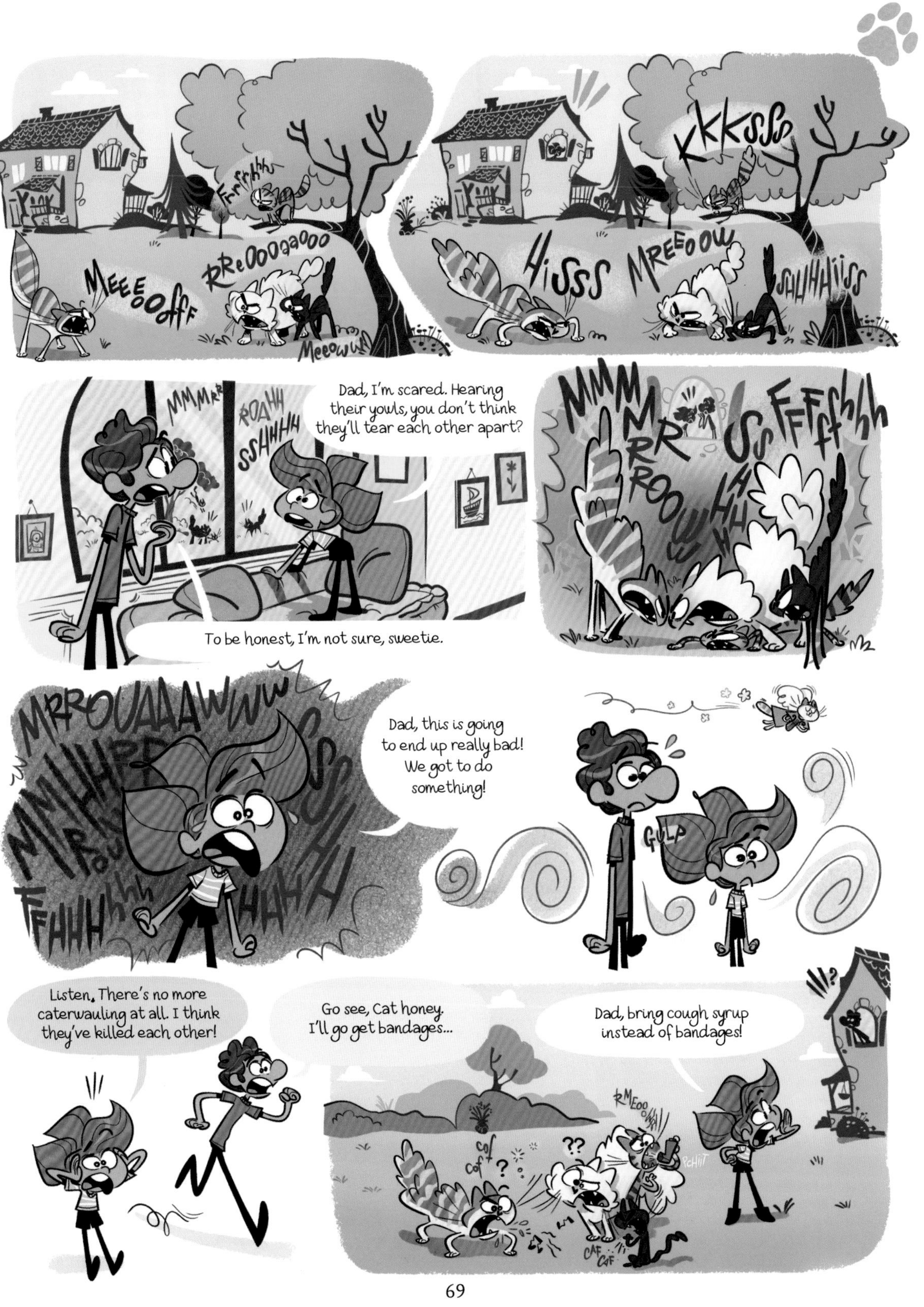
Frrrfhhh
MEEEOOFFF
RREOOOAAOOO
MEEOWW
KKKSSS
HISSS
MREEOOW
SHHHHISS
MMMRR
ROAHH
SSHHHH
Dad, I'm scared. Hearing their yowls, you don't think they'll tear each other apart?
To be honest, I'm not sure, sweetie.
MMMMRRROOWHHHH
SSFFFFfhhh
MRROUAAAWWW
Dad, this is going to end up really bad! We got to do something!
GULP
Listen. There's no more caterwauling at all. I think they've killed each other!
Go see, Cat honey. I'll go get bandages...
Dad, bring cough syrup instead of bandages!
RMEOOWW
PCHIIT
COF COF
??
CAF CAF

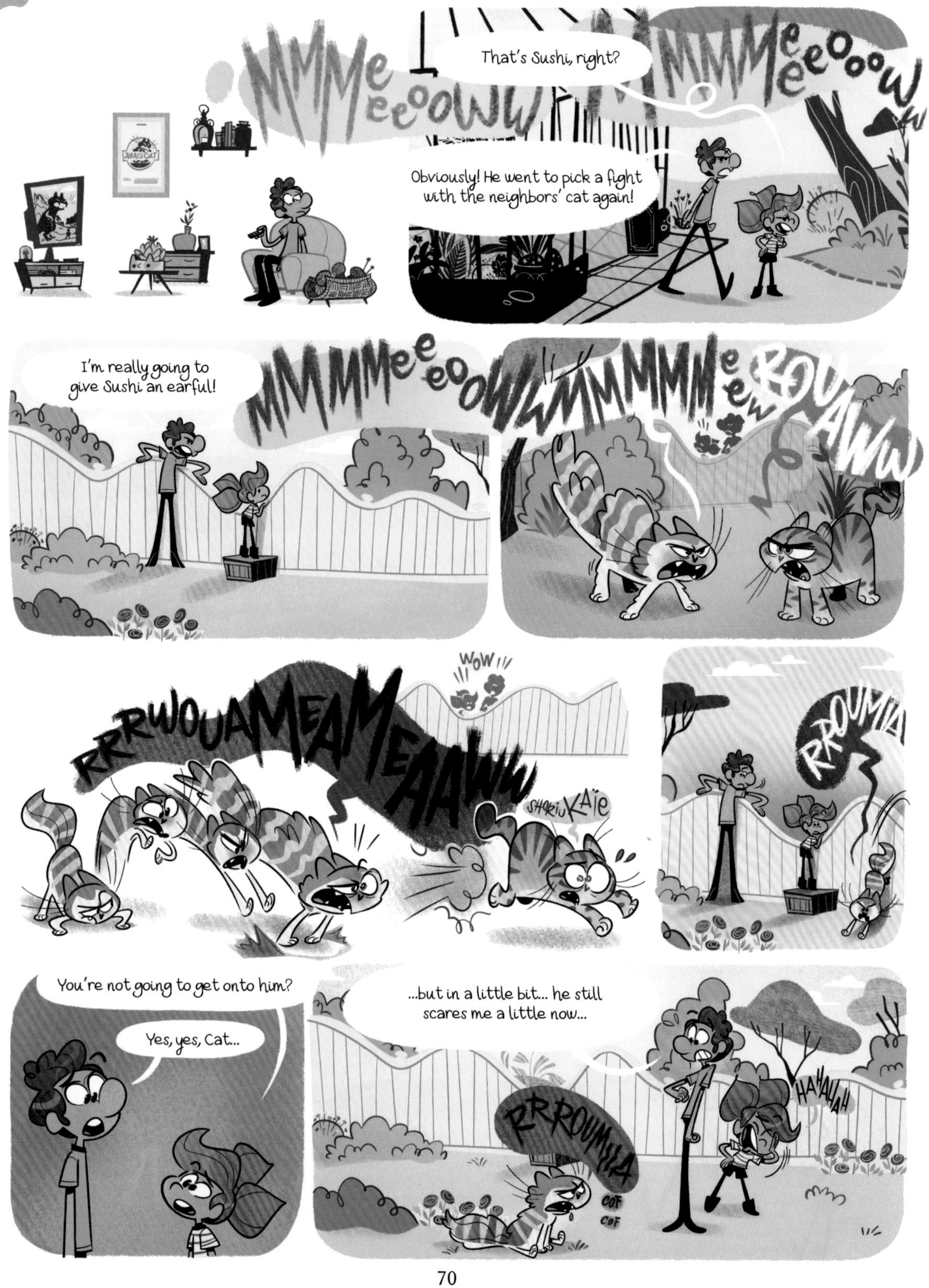
MMMeeeoOWW
That's Sushi, right?
MMMMeeeOooww
Obviously! He went to pick a fight with the neighbors' cat again!
I'm really going to give Sushi an earful!
MMMMeeeoOWW
MMMMMeew
RRRWOUAMEAMEAAWW
WOW
SHERIUKAÏE
RRROUMIA
You're not going to get onto him?
Yes, yes, Cat...
...but in a little bit... he still scares me a little now...
RRROUMIIA
COF COF
HAHAHAH

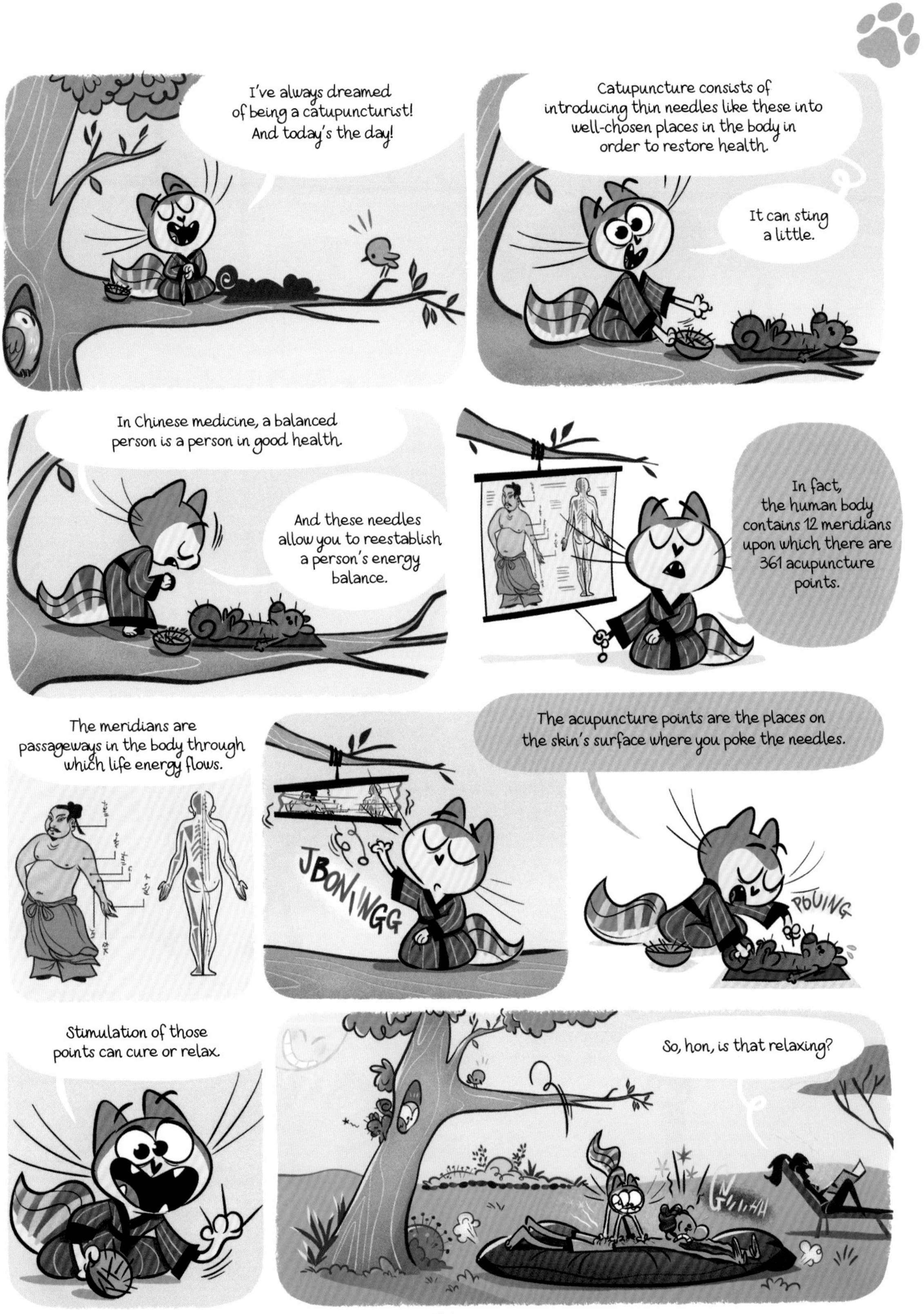
I've always dreamed of being a catupuncturist! And today's the day!
Catupuncture consists of introducing thin needles like these into well-chosen places in the body in order to restore health.
It can sting a little.
In Chinese medicine, a balanced person is a person in good health.
And these needles allow you to reestablish a person's energy balance.
In fact, the human body contains 12 meridians upon which there are 361 acupuncture points.
The meridians are passageways in the body through which life energy flows.
JBONNNGG
The acupuncture points are the places on the skin's surface where you poke the needles.
POUING
Stimulation of those points can cure or relax.
So, hon, is that relaxing?

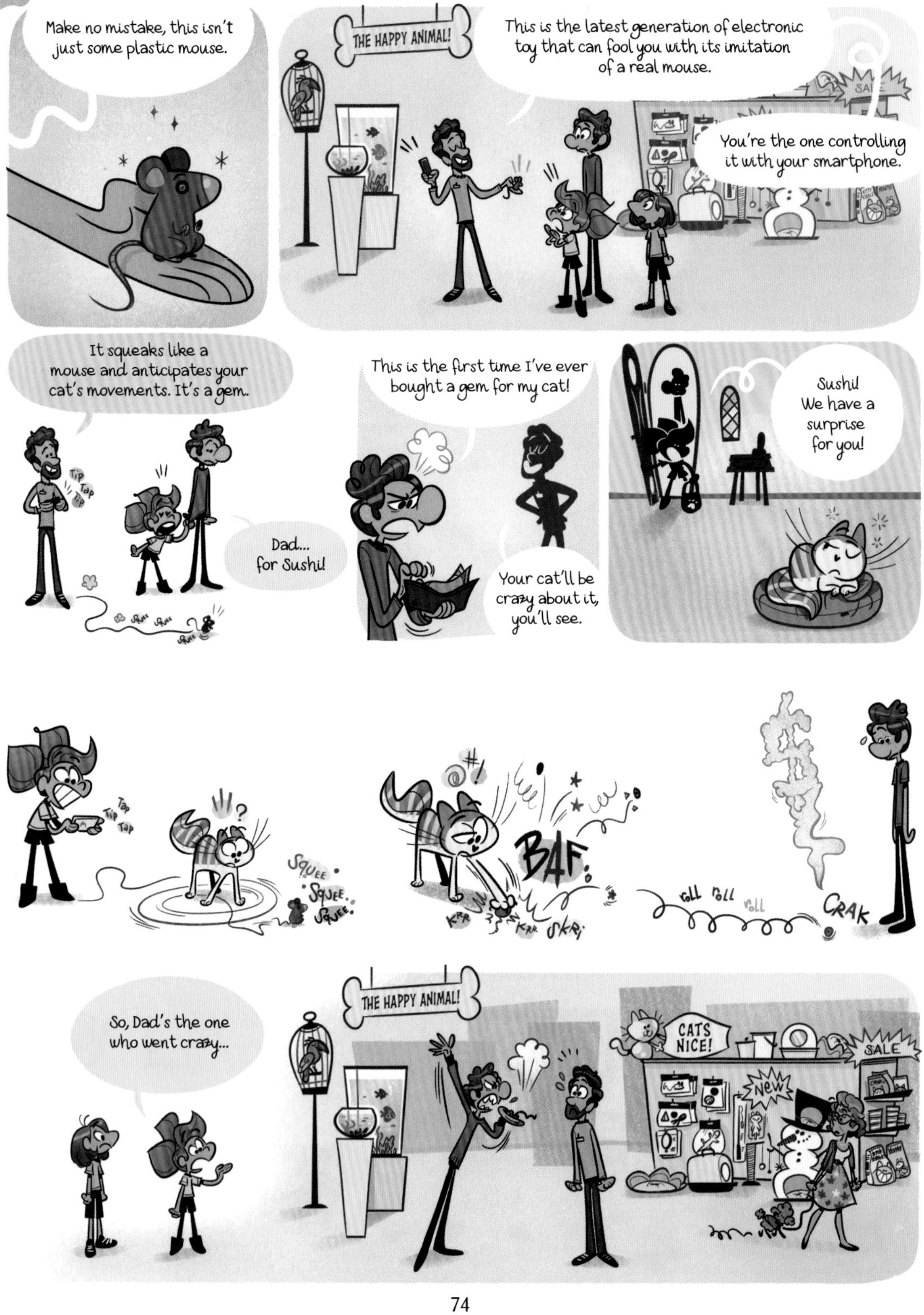

Make no mistake, this isn't just some plastic mouse.
THE HAPPY ANIMAL!
This is the latest generation of electronic toy that can fool you with its imitation of a real mouse.
You're the one controlling it with your smartphone.
SALE
It squeaks like a mouse and anticipates your cat's movements. It's a gem.
Tip Tap Tip
Dad... for Sushi!
SQUEE SQUEE SQUEE
This is the first time I've ever bought a gem for my cat!
Your cat'll be crazy about it, you'll see.
Sushi! We have a surprise for you!
Tip Tap Tap
SQUEE SQUEE SQUEE
BAF
KRR KRR SKRI
roll roll roll
CRAK
So, Dad's the one who went crazy...
THE HAPPY ANIMAL!
CATS NICE!
NEW
SALE

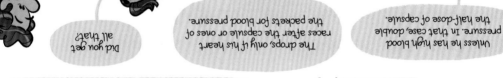

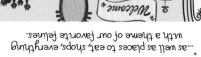
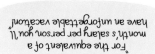

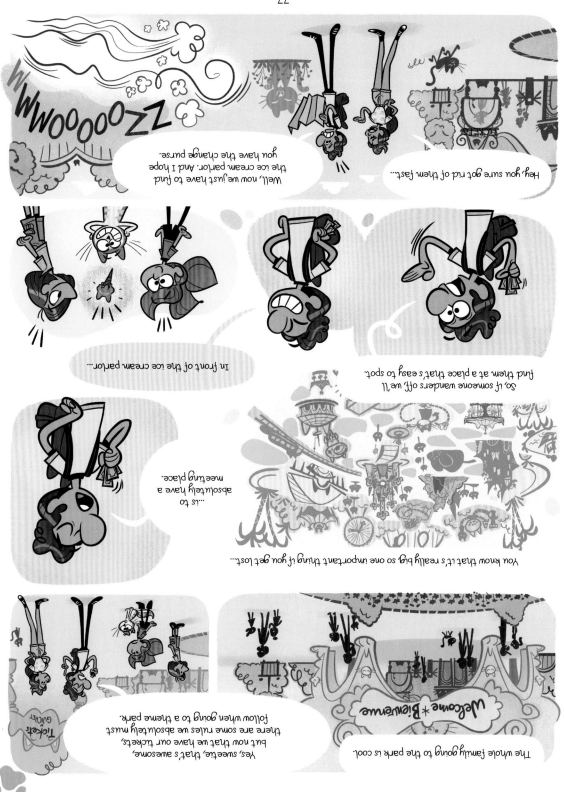

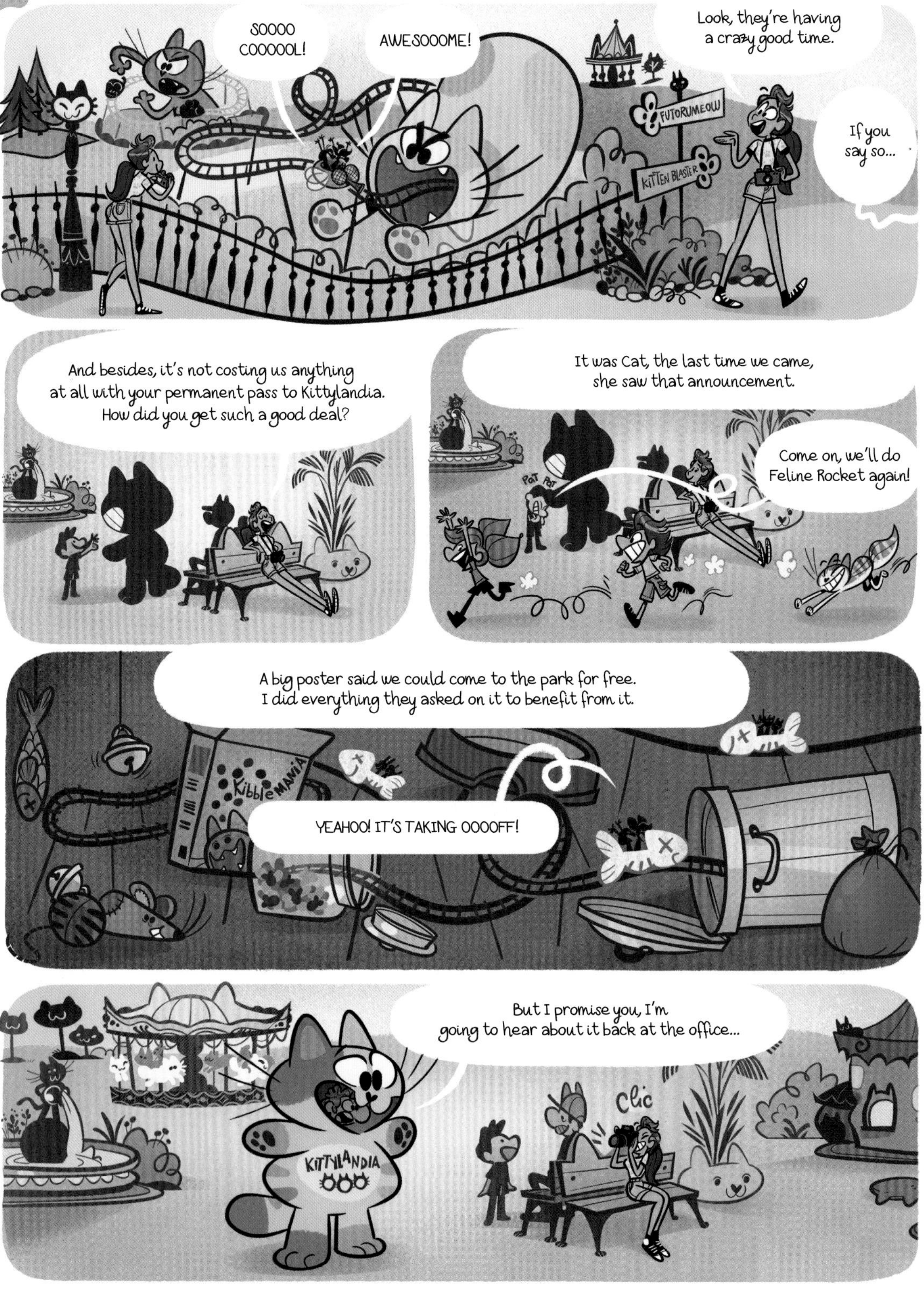
SOOOO COOOOOL!
AWESOOOME!
Look, they're having a crazy good time.
FUTORUMEOW
KITTEN BLASTER
If you say so...
And besides, it's not costing us anything at all with your permanent pass to Kittylandia. How did you get such a good deal?
It was Cat, the last time we came, she saw that announcement.
Come on, we'll do Feline Rocket again!
PAT PAT
A big poster said we could come to the park for free. I did everything they asked on it to benefit from it.
KibbleMANIA
YEAHOO! IT'S TAKING OOOOFF!
But I promise you, I'm going to hear about it back at the office...
Clic
KITTYLANDIA

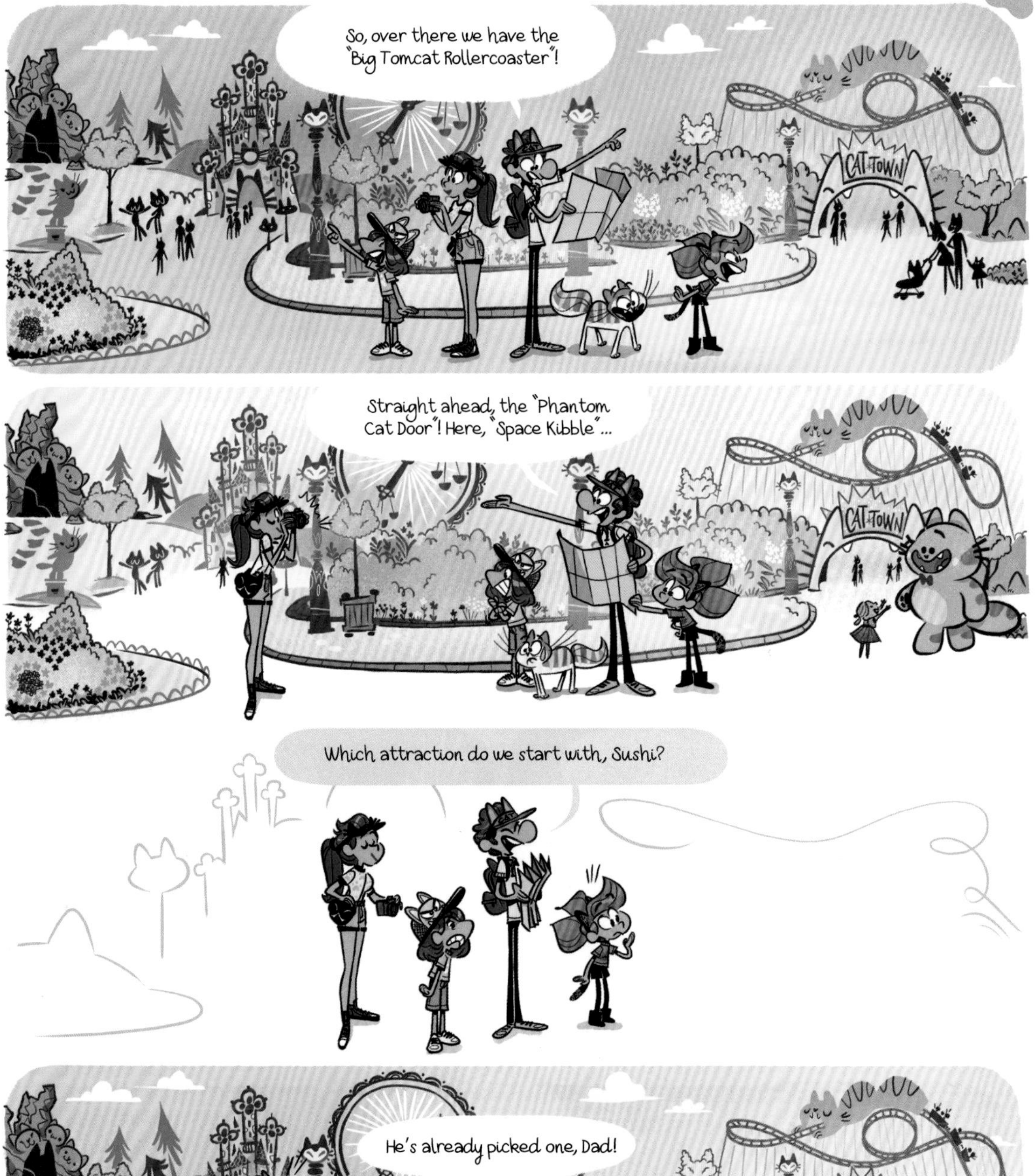
So, over there we have the "Big Tomcat Rollercoaster"!
CAT TOWN
Straight ahead, the "Phantom Cat Door"! Here, "Space Kibble"...
CAT TOWN
Which attraction do we start with, Sushi?
He's already picked one, Dad!
CAT TOWN

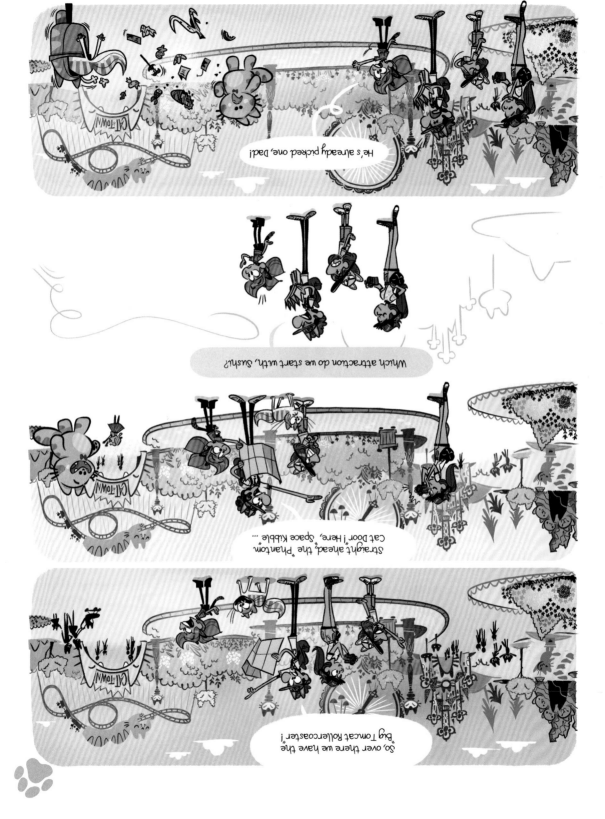

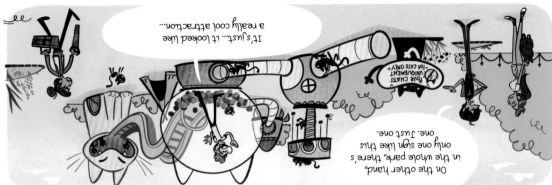

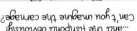

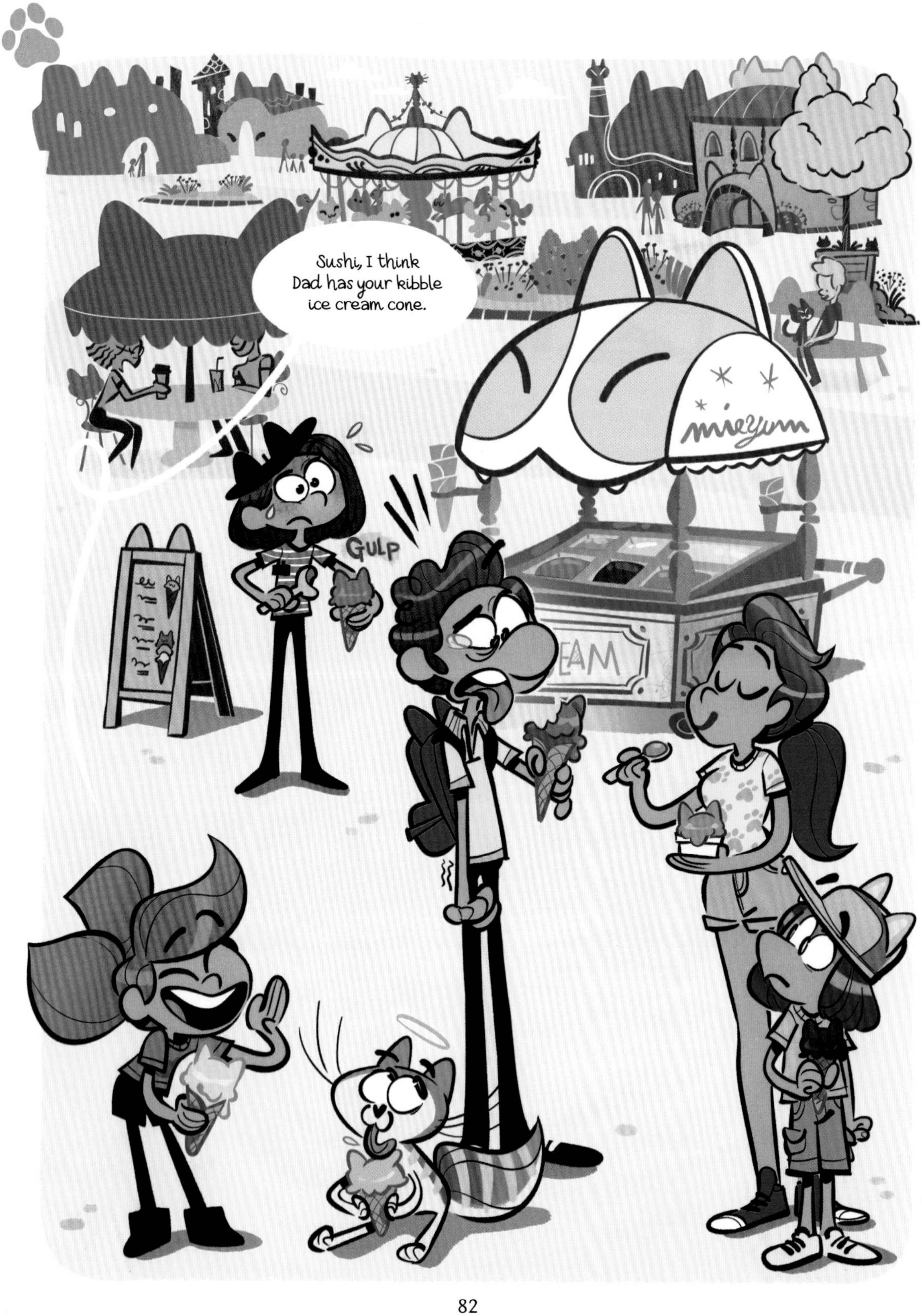
Sushi, I think Dad has your kibble ice cream cone.
GULP
mieyum
EAM

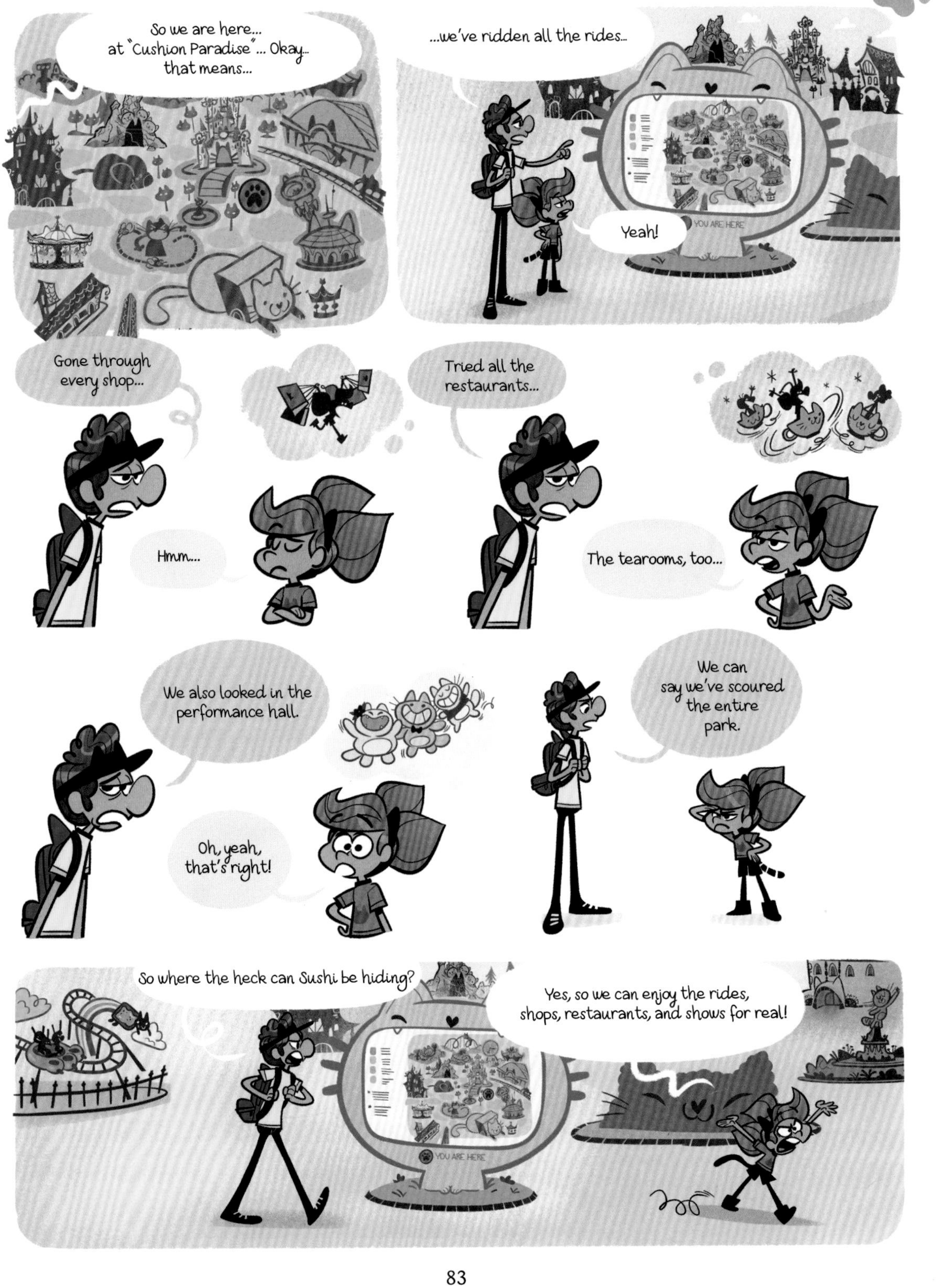
So we are here... at "Cushion Paradise"... Okay... that means...
...we've ridden all the rides...
Yeah!
YOU ARE HERE
Gone through every shop...
Hmm...
Tried all the restaurants...
The tearooms, too...
We also looked in the performance hall.
Oh, yeah, that's right!
We can say we've scoured the entire park.
So where the heck can Sushi be hiding?
Yes, so we can enjoy the rides, shops, restaurants, and shows for real!
YOU ARE HERE

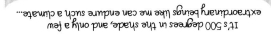

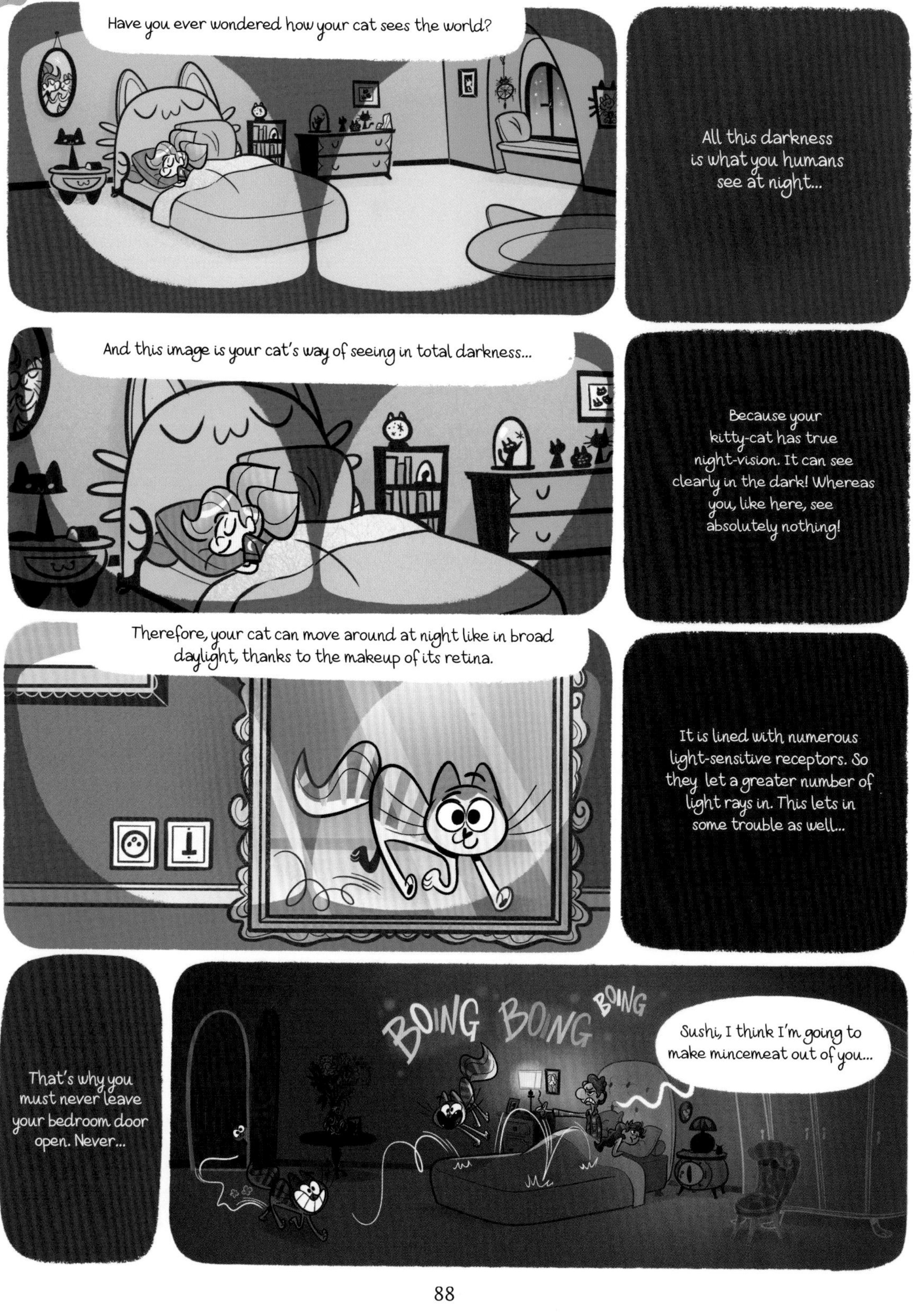
Have you ever wondered how your cat sees the world?
All this darkness is what you humans see at night...
And this image is your cat's way of seeing in total darkness...
Because your kitty-cat has true night-vision. It can see clearly in the dark! Whereas you, like here, see absolutely nothing!
Therefore, your cat can move around at night like in broad daylight, thanks to the makeup of its retina.
It is lined with numerous light-sensitive receptors. So they let a greater number of light rays in. This lets in some trouble as well...
That's why you must never leave your bedroom door open. Never...
BOING BOING BOING
Sushi, I think I'm going to make mincemeat out of you...

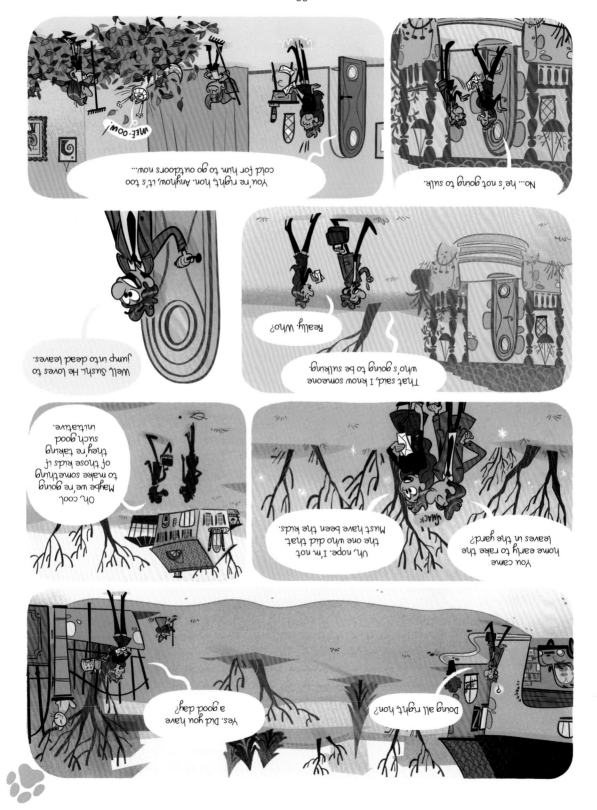

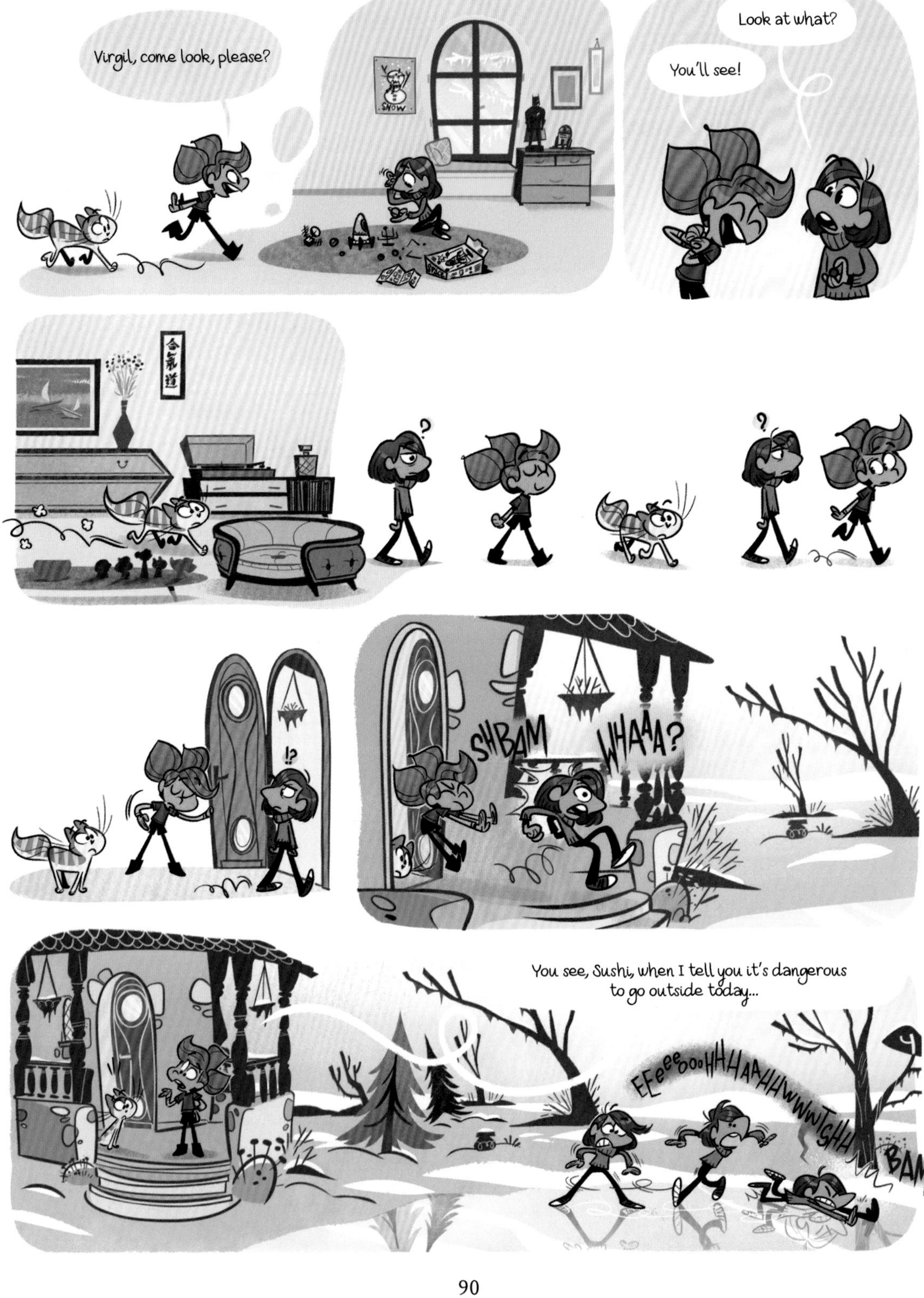
Virgil, come look, please?
Look at what?
You'll see!
!?
SHBAM
WHAAA?
You see, Sushi, when I tell you it's dangerous to go outside today...
EEeeeoooHHHAAHHWWWTSHH
BAM

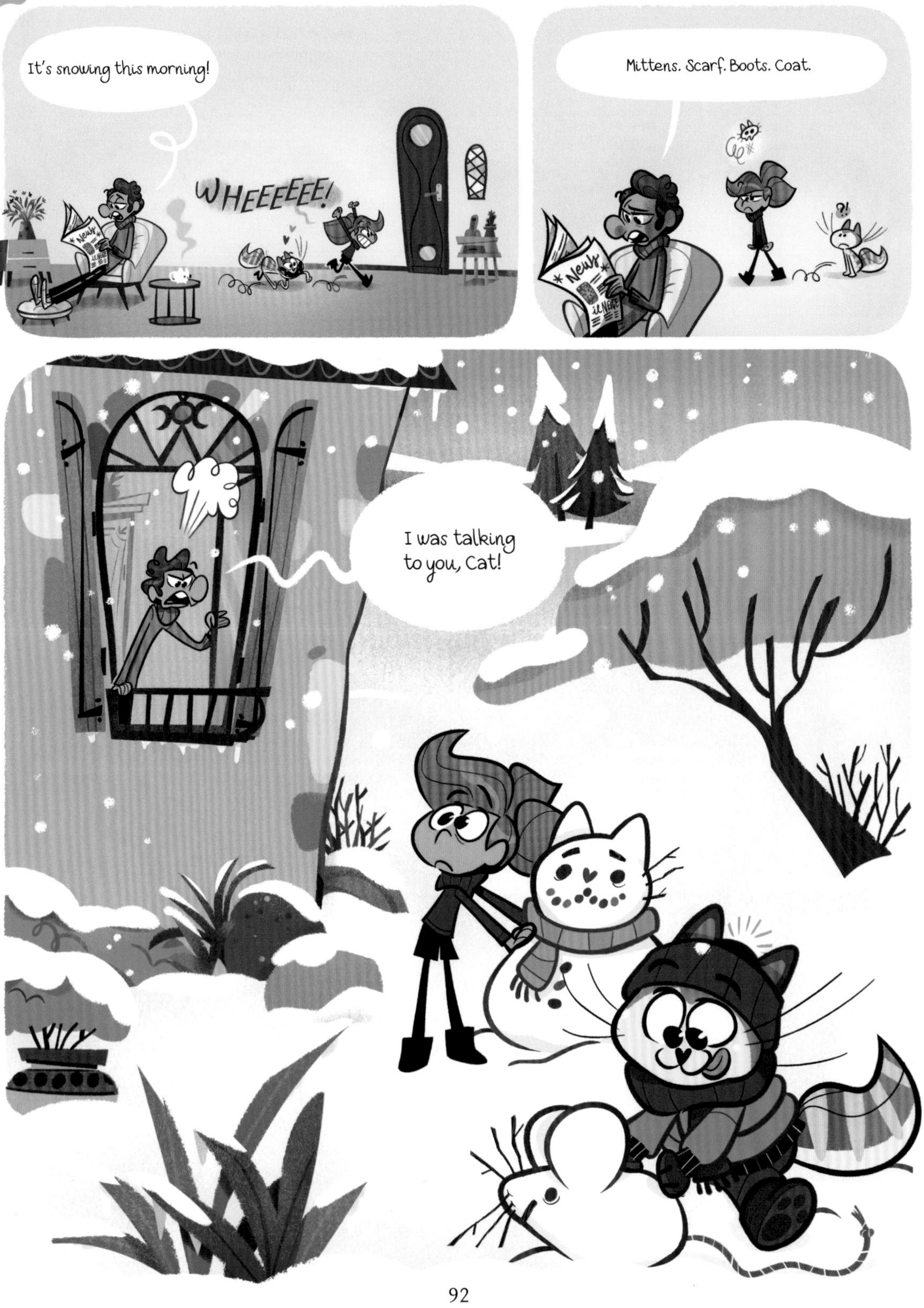
It's snowing this morning!
WHEEEEEE!
Mittens. Scarf. Boots. Coat.
I was talking to you, Cat!

WATCH OUT FOR PAPERCUTZ™

Welcome to the fear-fraught fourth CAT & CAT graphic novel by Christophe Cazenove and Hervé Richez, writers, and Yrgane Ramon, artist, from Papercutz, those fearless folks dedicated to publishing great graphic novels for all ages. I'm Jim Salicrup, Editor-in-Chief and a big fraidy cat, too!

Not long ago I rode the Wonder Wheel at Coney Island, and made the mistake of choosing the cars that swing while the big wheel goes round and round. Let me tell you—they should rename that ride the Terror Wheel, as far as I'm concerned. I'm not kidding. I was really scared as I rode what I thought was a "baby ride" because it seemed very likely I'd fall out of that ride, as it seemed very flimsy to me. It should be noted I left the ride totally safe and unharmed despite my fears.

That frightening experience came back to me when I recently read "What Goes Up" in THE LOUD HOUSE Summer Special #1 graphic novel from Papercutz, based on the hit Nickelodeon animated series. Lincoln Loud's friend Ronnie Anne Santiago goes to an amusement park with her dad, and even though he's terrified of many of the rides, he agrees to go on the Ferris wheel with her, and here's a peek at some of what happens…

do you suppose the title of this graphic novel is referring to him and not Sushi?

Kittylandia isn't the first crazy theme park to appear in a Papercutz graphic novel. Do you remember when Stephen Cling built Kakieland right next door to the HOTEL TRANSYLVANIA to drive them out, so that he could make it his own hotel for the theme park's guests? If not, just pick up either HOTEL TRANSYLVANIA #1 or HOTEL TRANSYLVANIA 3 IN 1 #1 for the full story. It features all your favorite monstrous characters from the hit film series in all-new stories that we're sure you'll enjoy.

Believe it or not there actually are several theme parks based on characters published by Papercutz. There are three (count 'em) Smurfs theme parks scattered around the world. And there's an Asterix theme park just north of Paris, France. There are Nickelodeon theme parks too, in the Mall of America and in New Jersey. But in a crazy way, I see Papercutz as a sort of theme park and each of our graphic novels is a fantastic ride. Whether it's the rollercoaster thrills of titles with larger-than-life characters such as DINOSAUR EXPLORERS and THE MYTHICS or the fun of such lovable characters such as THE FUZZY BASEBALL team (the Fernwood Valley Fuzzies) or THE GEEKY F@B 5, there's always lots of thrilling fun and excitement to be found in your favorite Papercutz graphic novels. Just check out the preview of the totally strange ATTACK OF THE STUFF "The Life and Times of Bill Waddler," preview on the following pages. This graphic novel, created by best-selling author Jim Benton, is guaranteed to be unlike any graphic novel you ever read before.

Be sure to get the full story in THE LOUD HOUSE Summer Special #1, available now at booksellers and libraries everywhere.

When Cat, her dad Nat, Sam, Virgil, and Sushi visit Kittylandia it doesn't really seem that scary, although note the only one scared on the cover is Nathan… Gee,

Thanks,

Jim

STAY IN TOUCH!

EMAIL: salicrup@papercutz.com
WEB: www.papercutz.com
TWITTER: @papercutzgn
INSTAGRAM: @papercutzgn
FACEBOOK: PAPERCUTZGRAPHICNOVELS
FANMAIL: Papercutz, 160 Broadway, Suite 700, East Wing, New York, NY 10038
Go to papercutz.com and sign up for the free Papercutz e-newsletter!

SPECIAL PREVIEW OF

ATTACK OF THE STUFF

"The Life and Times of Bill Waddler"

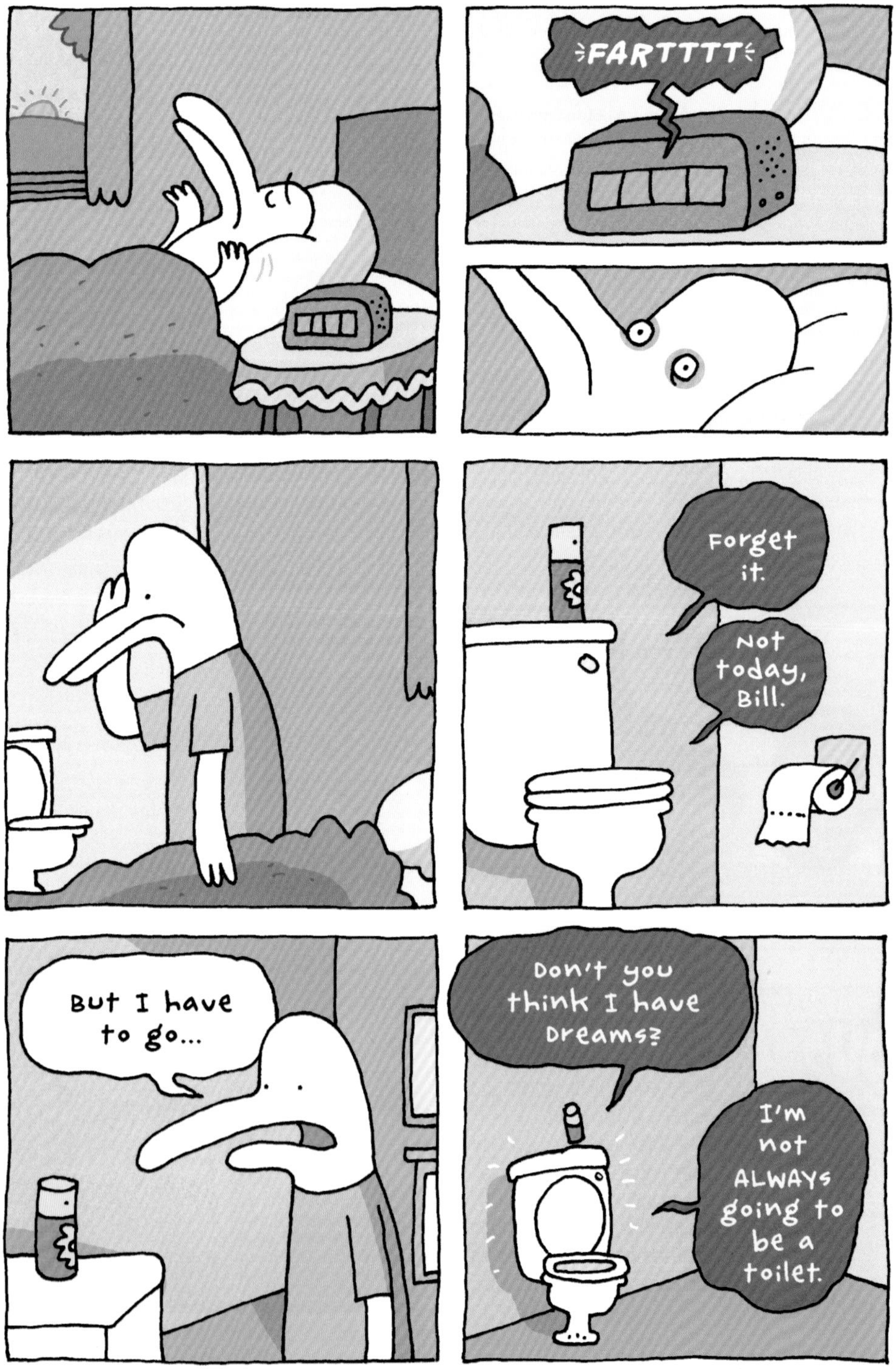
FARTTTT
Forget it.
Not today, Bill.
But I have to go...
Don't you think I have Dreams?
I'm not ALWAYS going to be a toilet.

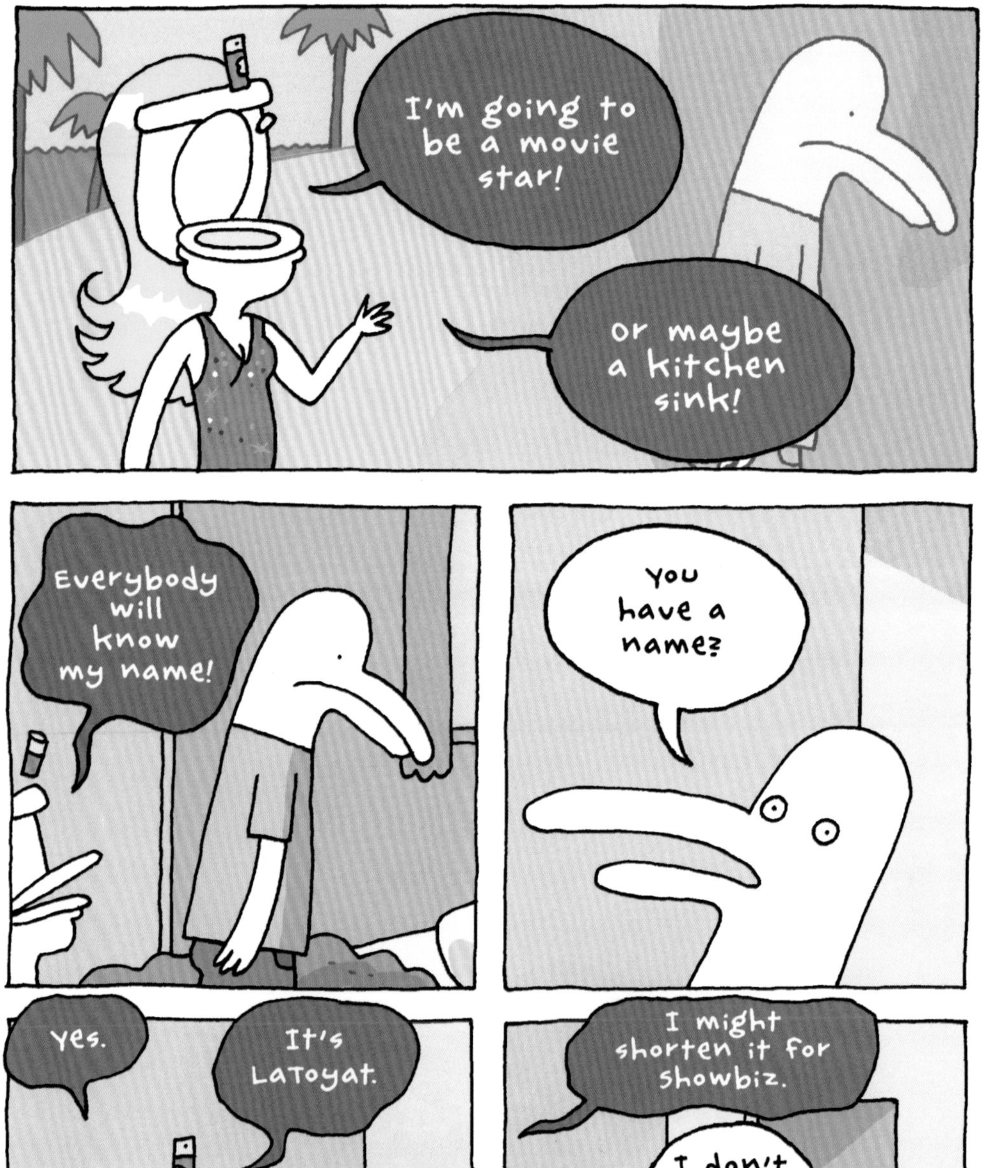
I'm going to be a movie star!
or maybe a kitchen sink!
Everybody will know my name!
you have a name?
yes.
It's Latoyat.
Latoyat Toiletstein.
I might shorten it for showbiz.
I don't have time for this.

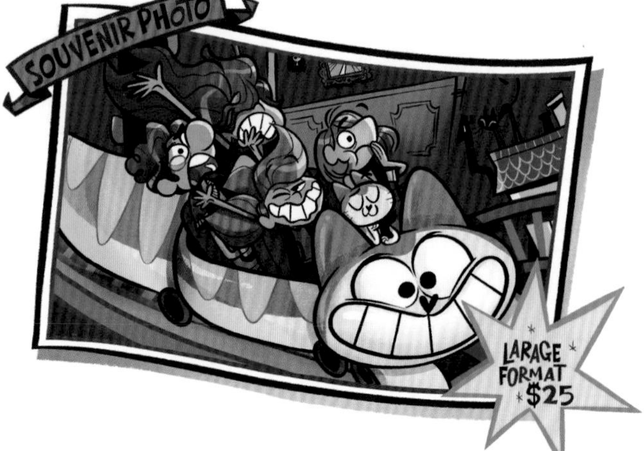
SOUVENIR PHOTO
LARAGE FORMAT $25